To Jordyn, for the ceaseless waves of faith and
encouragement. For the love that reminds me daily that I
am one of the lucky ones.

To Mom, for seeing something in me at a young age that
I didn't truly appreciate until I was much older.

And Jesus answering said, A certain man went down from Jerusalem to Jericho, and fell among thieves, which stripped him of his raiment, and wounded him, and departed, leaving him half dead.

And by chance there came down a certain priest that way: and when he saw him, he passed by on the other side.

And likewise a Levite, when he was at the place, came and looked on him, and passed by on the other side.

But a certain Samaritan, as he journeyed, came where he was: and when he saw him, he had compassion on him, And went to him, and bound up his wounds, pouring in oil and wine, and set him on his own beast, and brought him to an inn, and took care of him.

Which now of these three, thinkest thou, was neighbour unto him that fell among the thieves? And He said, he that showed mercy on him. Then said Jesus unto him,

Go, and do thou likewise.

Luke 10: 30-34, 36-37

Prologue

It was hot. She remembered that. Above all else, in that place it was a sweltering sort of heat that suffocated you as soon as you walked in. There's something about a room like that; a space that creates such a prison of discomfort that you can't flee even from your senses much less physically escape. But, she supposed, that was the point.

Sarah, now sixteen years old and living her best life as yet another product of the system, was currently living out her second year as a foster child. She was quiet and kept to herself, a fact well known among the other girls in this particular group home. They had made little effort to accept her as one of their own which suited her just fine, having learned long ago that these relationships were temporary at best.

Her black hair, cut just above shoulder length, was pressed against the wall of her room just next to her bed. She often hid there, between her bed and the corner, so that she could simulate some form of privacy. Perhaps, she thought, if the other girls had no direct line of sight then she would be in her own space; her own little home in a world where no such personal luxuries would ever exist. She was safe there.

But it had been hot, that night so long ago now. Sarah had forgotten very little about the day that her father went missing. Even at the young age of only ten years old she had been able to appreciate the lifting of that burden. Little girls are meant to lean upon their fathers and look to them for protection. Little girls are not meant to fear their fathers, ten year olds should know that their home is safe. But Sarah had reached an entirely premature level of clarity by a very young age and had, as happens so often, grown up too fast. Her father was a villain, so when her father went missing no tears were shed. She remembered that feeling of relief, the overwhelming release from her pain that came the moment she knew he was gone.

When fear is all you know, freedom is a very powerful thing.

So now, in her safe space of complete solitude, she thought back on how she earned her freedom. There had been a hero. Sarah had only met the man once but she knew every curve of his face, the striking color of his eyes, the rhythm at which his feet walked across that old wooden floor. He had come to her shortly after her father went missing and asked her to make a choice.

That nightmarish place where terrible things had happened, that was his home or so she thought. Yet somehow, in that space where people had died in the very worst way, she felt safe. The stranger ushered her into a large, dimly lit room where the shadows seemed to take on a life of their own. He had taken her father and brought him there to be punished.

Sarah thought back to that choice. How many little girls have been challenged to choose their father's fate? Really, how much of their own fate did any child ever control?

The group home was quiet at night. As much as her therapist (generously paid for by the county) tried to get Sarah to open up, these moments at night in her private space were the only times that she reached this level of sincerity and clarity. Sarah supposed that despite her resistance, there was likely some credence to the therapist's dogma. While she had never revealed to anyone the true circumstances surrounding her father's disappearance, she felt sure that her young mind was still learning to comprehend the very extreme circumstances that led to her becoming an orphan.

In the end, she did make a choice. In very simple terms, Sarah chose to have her father murdered. The stranger offered her that, in fact he presented it to her almost as simply as if she were choosing between two options at a restaurant: life or death? Her choice to put her father to death had never been second guessed, that was easy even as a little girl. The greatest challenge she faced in the days following was the surprisingly difficult question - what now?

In the end, she supposed, that is what led her to this home. There she was in this corner of this house in this particular part of town with these particular people. But none of that really mattered to her. What mattered was him- the stranger. Who was he? Why had he done what he did and where did he go?

Sarah climbed into her bed from her private space on the floor as she did every night. She laid her head on her pillow and closed her eyes. This night she would dream of the man who saved her just as she had done every night for the last two years.

There she lay, safe. Alone. As she always would be.

Chapter 1

It was quite famous at one point, the media couldn't get enough of "The Good Samaritan Killer." At the time it wasn't hard to connect the dots, the killer went out of his way to provide all the evidence needed to not only convict his victims but to embarrass the authorities for their apparent inability to do their jobs.

As happens so often in American media, the sensational story eventually quietly faded into the uninteresting. The Good Samaritan was a staple among all streaming documentaries about serial killers and unsolved mysteries but it had been so long since the stories were reported in the mainstream media that they almost fell into local folklore. Time is forgetful and the short attention span of the modern American can be quite forgiving.

It would seem that this is how The Good Samaritan was able to continue killing for so long.

———————

Churches these days can be so cold by comparison to the grand cathedrals of the past. Every town is filled with parishioners who attend square meeting spaces replete with water fountains and handicapped restrooms. Father Ellis admired his home as he walked past the pews of his church, a rare gem in a modern world. The Blessed Heart Catholic Church was built just after the founding of the city, nestled right into the heart of downtown.

Parking was difficult but it was worth it to have the chance to worship in a place bursting with such history and tradition.

Father Ellis admired the stained-glass windows that lined the high walls of dark stone, each with their own story to tell. Far above him the ribbed vault met in an intricate pattern of diamonds that lined the cieling. When he had joined the seminary he had hoped to set down roots in a place such as this, his passion for the Lord and the teachings of Christ were his highest priority but a close second was his love of history. To spread the word in this gothic setting just as had been done for so many centuries before him was something of a special honor.

Well into his late sixties, Father Ellis had seen his flock change quite a bit over the years. These days the pews were often filled with elderly crowds where once there were so many youthful faces. Young families, however, were not completely a thing of the past. In fact, Father Ellis was on his way to a standing appointment with one of his youngest church members. He approached the rear of the sanctuary and paused to admire the confessional before him. The classical wooden design with intricate carvings that a craftsman had labored over so long ago never failed to impress him. He smiled with pride as he opened his door and gently shut it behind him.

It had been a long walk and Father Ellis took a breath before continuing. He brushed his thinning, gray hair back before sliding the partition over. Through the wicker mesh he could see a young girl. Fifteen year old Lisa Harper sat upright with excellent posture. Her long, dishwater blonde hair was tied in a pony tail and cascaded over a dark dress peppered with small flowers. She stared at her feet and did not react to the partition sliding open.

"Hello, Lisa," Father Ellis said with a smile. The silence that followed was unusually long and unsettling.

"Forgive me, Father, for I have sinned," her voice was calm once she finally spoke. Father Ellis noted that something was different about her demeanor.

"How long since your last confession, child?"

"Nine days."

Her eyes still fixated on the floor beneath her, she barely seemed to acknowledge his presence. Father Ellis smiled, he knew Lisa well and losing track of time was one of her few vices.

"You missed bible study this week" he teased.

"I know. I'm sorry. That's the reason that I'm here."

He thought back to the days when her young family had first joined the church. Lisa was only seven and she was filled with such passion and eagerness to know God. She had been the youngest of just three children that attended Sunday school on a regular basis. It brought him great joy to see her eyes light up when hearing the stories of the Bible.

"There was a time, Lisa, when you were excited to come to church."

"Sometimes things change, Father." she said coldly.

He smiled, young people can be wiser than one might assume. "Yes they do. Tell me your troubles."

Lisa paused, she took a deep breath.

"I have had inappropriate relations with a man," she confessed.

This grabbed the priest's attention. Lisa's confessions of this nature were relatively common. He was glad for the opportunity to be a guiding light in her world which sometimes seemed so confusing and dark.

"Again?" Father Ellis' tone had shifted to that of a disappointed parent.

"Yes, Father," she admitted while still showing a remarkable lack of emotion and still staring at the grains in the wooden floor at her feet.

"And do you understand that it is sinful to do such a thing?"

Lisa waited for a moment to consider the question. Of course, the answer was obvious, but there was something about it that gave her pause. Still, she studied the wooden grain at her feet that flowed and snaked like a river.

"Yes. I am ashamed," her obligatory answer finally came. Father Ellis nodded his head in agreement.

"Premarital relations are a sin. God is always watching, Lisa. But I can help you."

"I don't want your help," she quietly snapped back at him. The sudden change in tone caused Father Ellis to take a sharp breath.

"You can't go through this alone, my child."

Disregarding her priest's words, Lisa continued. Her words came slowly, deliberately.

"A man came to me, said he knew what was happening to me. He told me that I didn't have to live my life this way."

Father Ellis was growing concerned, he shifted in his seat. Suddenly his partition felt smaller and warmer, closing in around him like a coffin.

"What are you talking about? What man?" he asked.

Outside the confessional, the beautiful classically designed gothic church had many features Father Ellis would often brag about to anyone who would listen. One of the very best features, in his opinion, was the comfortable, soft carpet that lined the aisle between the pews. It was so forgiving that your footsteps made not a sound as you walked down the aisle. On this day, a man walked down the aisle unnoticed by Father Ellis.

This silent stranger wore a black suit complete with a thin black tie. His striking blue eyes were on the confessional doors as he approached. The lights from the hanging chandeliers reflected off his blonde hair as he passed each one.

Lisa continued her confession, "A stranger. He said that I didn't need to be afraid anymore and that it wasn't my fault."

Father Ellis found this way of talking to be very strange, foreign even. She did not wait for him to respond, "He said he found me, that he knew what was happening to me...he could see it in my eyes..."

"You don't even know this man," Father Ellis exclaimed.

"That's why I trust him. He told me that I deserve better, that my life should be better. And that he would help me make right what was wrong. He would punish those who have hurt me."

His lip quivering, Father Ellis pleaded, "Punish? Lisa, what you're talking about is not legal! Not only in the laws of man, but in the laws of God!"

By this time she seemed to ignore the words of her priest entirely. She had come here to say something important and no clamoring or misdirection was going to stop her.

"So, I told him something that I had never told anyone before."

"Please, Lisa, this is between you and God…" he said with tears forming in his eyes.

Lisa finally raised her head and turned towards the old man. Her hazel eyes pierced through the mesh partition and struck such a terror in him that he pulled away from the small window. In her he saw a little girl no more, something had changed. Just inches away from him he saw a vengeful spirit.

"I told him about you," she growled.

Suddenly, Father Ellis's door slammed open with a loud crash that echoed through the old chambers. The Good Samaritan towered over the man, standing a staggering six foot, five inches in height. The priest yelped in fear as two large hands reached into the confessional and ripped him out like a dog being dragged by the collar.

The door slammed shut and Lisa jumped slightly at the deafening sound. She remained fixated on the now empty compartment across from her until finally a tear formed and slid down her cheek. It was done.

Chapter 2

It had been a while since Detective John Corbin had gotten a full night's sleep. He was in decent shape and capable of the physical demands of being a cop but it took a toll on his ability to maintain a healthy and well balanced lifestyle. A black detective on the force wasn't as rare as it once was but a physically fit middle aged cop of any color was like a shooting star.

Corbin sat at his desk, lost in a maze of his own making. His colleagues saw him as obsessive, wanting to respect his commitment but refusing to admit he was right. For years now, this lone detective had been committed to a string of murders known as "The Good Samaritan Killings", a term with which the media had christened the glorified vigilante. Choosing to commit to this case was no small decision, having now immersed himself in years of inconclusive investigations, testimonies and scraps of evidence. Today was just one more day of praying for any semblance of progress in what even he had begun to tell himself was a lost cause.

On this day, the lucky winner was camera number DOT-051590 located on the sunny side of Mulberry and Ash Street. Unfortunately, the vigilante was smart enough to maintain a constant variety when dumping his victims outside police stations and other government buildings. In the days prior to this video clip coming across Corbin's desk, a body had been dumped at a fire station on Mulberry accompanied with the typical collection of ironclad evidence neatly placed into a box. Corbin couldn't honestly recall which victim this was or what their crime was, but the one silver lining was that the camera at the corner managed to catch a partial view of his suspect.

The enigma of a serial killer could be seen through the driver's side window, his face partially obscured not only by shadow but the door frame of the vehicle. In an ocean of completely useless surveillance footage, this new clip did not provide any new information but could at least confirm a thing or two. The man was caucasian, most likely between 35 and 60 and by all accounts a sharp dresser. Just about every clip the killer had ever been seen in found him sporting a business suit, always black and always clean.

Detective Corbin glanced across his desk. He knew a few Type A kids back in high school that would have a panic attack if they could see him now. Something about the mob of photographs and documents that scattered their way across his workspace made sense to him and in the end, that was all that mattered. The photographs all shared a common aesthetic; grainy and out of focus featuring the same pale faced man who refused to reveal his full countenance as if he knew where every camera in the city was placed. They had a haunting quality to them, Corbin had learned to keep from staring at them for too long after he thought he saw an image move on more than one occasion.

"Yo!" Corbin was snapped back to reality by a younger detective, Victor Jackson, who recently earned his new rank. "Hey, we're all going out for drinks tonight. Wad'ya say?" Jackson asked, already knowing the answer.

Corbin clicked the image on his screen, zooming into the mysterious face as he forced a response, "What did I say last time?" He took a moment to remind himself that teaching young detectives the ropes was a good and important part of how the department worked. It didn't do much good to fixate on the inconvenience of being assigned a member of Gen Z as a partner.

"Oh, sorry, I thought that you might have had that stick up your ass removed since last time." Jackson still had a thing or two to learn about the difference between friendly ball-busting and insubordination. Corbin ignored the comment and Jackson took a closer look at the image on the screen, "What intersection is that?"

"Mulberry and Ash, that fire house," Corbin answered.

Jackson glanced across the anxiety attack that was Corbin's desk. "Well, it'll make a fine addition to the collection, definitely digging the vibe you've got going here. Really, you should think about some sort of grainy creepy guy wallpaper line. Bed Bath and Beyond, some place like that, it'd be huge."

"Fuck off." Corbin had passed the point that he was willing to tolerate this particular brand of idiot.

Jackson, seemingly admitting defeat, moved past Corbin's desk and stepped towards the squad room exit. The young detective stopped and turned back. "Hey, Corbin," Jackson began "have you ever asked yourself why you stay here alone all night working on that case?"

This was easy to ignore. Corbin quickly counted in his head the number of times his commitment to The Good Samaritan file had been questioned.

"Because if any other cop in the city saw the guy who caps off rapists and murderers in a bar they'd buy him a beer." Jackson waited a moment, curious to see if that comment would elicit a response. Hearing only the continued typing of a lonely man, Jackson shook his head and walked out the door.

With the empty squad room to himself, Corbin opened a folder on his desktop and a large library of video clips loaded onto the screen. There hadn't been many people willing to come forward about the vigilante, this collection featured the entirety of those who had been convinced to make a statement. Some of the videos were from before Corbin had joined the case, back when pursuing the suspect was less of an indicator of a dead end career. The thumbnails that spread across his screen looked like a Guess Who board of poor choices. No one wanted to be there or be making these statements and everyone sported a look that said they wished they could have the last several years of their life back.

When talking about individuals associated with the killer one had to divide them into two distinct categories. These categories were difficult to define as they were, in fact, all victims. First, you had the victims the killer had abducted, tortured and left nearly dead on some government building doorstep in the city. Technically speaking they were the lucky ones, The Good Samaritan seemed to prefer murder over leniency.

Next, you had his victim's victims. It was true, Corbin had to admit, that every person discovered to have fallen prey to The Good Samaritan whether they were dead or left alive had been proven a criminal in some way.

It had never been possible to directly link these people to the killer but it was widely assumed by the authorities and media alike that the abductions and subsequent torture/killings were a coordinated effort between "Good Sam" and those that had been subjected to some sort of abuse or other crime. Proving conspiracy to commit murder or kidnapping had its challenges but nothing like this had ever been seen in the history of the department. With very little exception it had been impossible to prove that any one person ever worked directly with the killer and certainly those who were suspected never admitted to any of it. It was an astounding amount of evidence to conceal for so many years leading some to suspect that the crimes may even be the work of someone within the city government.

Corbin scrolled through the clips while referencing a document next to his keyboard. Today's selection was file number 081419-48, a filing system that Corbin developed himself based on the date of the date of the recording followed by the number assigned to that particular incident associated with this case. The tired detective shook his head as he acknowledged how high that number, forty eight, really was and the fact that this file was now 4 years old.

He opened the file. The video quality was poor, the department had since invested in higher quality camera's making these old files look like eight millimeter film by comparison. Hidden amongst the grain and deep shadows on the screen was a man. With his hands on the table and his head slumped down it was hard to see his face clearly. What was easy to see, however, was what seemed like years of physical abuse this person had endured. Many of the scars across his neck and hands had been partially healed by time. Remnants of what looked like a chemical burn of some sort could be seen around the scars.

This interview had taken place long before Corbin took over the case, there was a long list of detectives who had put in their time and achieved little to no progress. Corbin noted the digital text in the corner of the screen, the man's name was Jeremy Lasiter. Jeremy seemed unable to control the shaking of his right hand as he answered the investigator's questions. Off camera, the detective's voice could be heard through the static hiss of the speakers. "Could you describe him?" he asked, seemingly not expecting a wildly different version of what he'd heard so many times before.

"He was tall, like uh ... over six feet, easy. Blue eyes, no scars or nothing." Jeremy answered, nervously.

The detective responded sympathetically, not easy to do knowing what this man had done. "It would be really helpful if we could set you up with a sketch artist."

"Fine, whatever you need. Just make it quick."

"We'll be as quick as we ca-"

The man threw his face into his hands. "I shouldn't even be here, I don't know why I'm here! He's just gonna fuckin' kill me."

"Well, you're going to jail. You know that. We went through the goodie bag that was left with you and I gotta say, it doesn't look good for you. But if you decide to help us, we can make it easier. And if you're worried about your safety, we can protect you."

"Yeah, sure."

The detective sat back, struggling with how to proceed. It was clear any details Jeremy was hiding behind those glassy eyes had been locked away in fear. "Can I ask you a question?" he said finally.

"That's what I'm here for, I guess." Jeremy looked defeated.

The detective took a look at the remaining questions he had scribbled on his notepad, bored of asking the same things every time. Suddenly, the he seemed exhausted with the same old routine. "Do you think you deserved all this?" he asked, staring at Jeremy's scars that would never fully heal.

Jeremy didn't answer right away but redirected his attention to his shaking hand. He studied the wounds that were visible for some time, knowing that so many others hid beneath his clothing, before looking back up at the detective to finally make eye contact and reveal the extensive scarring on his face. He broke his silence and spoke in a tone that seemed to judge the detective for his insolence.

"Of course I did."

Chapter 3

There are parts of every major city that time seems to politely ignore and allow to simply continue without change. At night this part of town seemed to soak up light at every corner. What few street lights there were shone straight down and refused to reveal the world around them.

On an uninteresting corner of an insignificant block there stood a building. Nearly identical to its surrounding structures, the large two story warehouse refused to be noticed, hiding in the shadows of the night. The block was silent except for the slow sound of a light breeze. Inside, however, screams had echoed off the old wooden walls for the last four days.

The interior of the massive structure was a hybrid of wood and steel. The second floor sported a balcony that stretched the inner circumference and looked down on the ground level. Mostly the space was occupied by the old bones of industry that used to serve this work place. Now the large machines and supply boxes existed only to collect dust and shadows. Everywhere you could feel a sense of terror that seemed to hover as an invisible mist. People had died there, the worst possible way. What was clear was that if you were in that particular room on this elusive block you didn't want to be.

At the center of the first floor there was a chair set on a wooden floor that was stained in every direction a very dark red that was nearly black. In this chair there sat a man, a broken shell of a priest who had spent the last few days at the mercy of his captor. The Good Samaritan revealed himself from the darkness, stepping into the large cone of light that shone down on the blood soaked center of the great hall.

The stranger, still dressed in a black suit, studied his work without emotion. The holy man sat there, strapped to the wooden chair that now had more coats of dried blood on it than could be counted. Father Ellis was screaming in pain, or at least he was to the very best of his abilities. With his head down the priest emitted a sort of weak whine of agony. Hope had left long ago. Now only the bleeding wounds that covered his naked body were there to remind him he was still alive. The constant pain his torturer had inflicted upon him was done with such precision that the dreadful sensations seemed to never fade.

The Good Samaritan approached a large wooden table placed just at the edge of the light. On it was a collection of tools that had been used for terrible things. He carefully stood beside it considering his options before picking up a chisel that had been filed into a blade. Deep footsteps approached Father Ellis as he closed his eyes and bowed his head in a moment of desperation.

"Oh Father," he mumbled "please protect me and watch over me in this my darkest hour..."

The Good Samaritan seemed almost offended that someone else was getting the priest's attention. Unwilling to wait any longer he plunged the chisel into his victim's knee, pushing deep into the tissue just above the knee cap. Father Ellis let out as much of a scream as he had left, his voice having been mostly lost within the first day of arriving. Cold blue eyes scanned the injury and the blood streaming from it then looked up to examine the pain on the old man's face.

The chisel did not twist easily, this area was home to a lot of bone and cartilage. By forcing the knee cap out from its resting place The Good Samaritan was able to achieve a ninety degree rotation. Again, the priest was studied and carefully considered. The man pulled back his suit sleeve to reveal a leather strapped watch with a gold rim and white face that had about three decades of wear on it.

Disappointed by what he learned from his time piece, The Good Samaritan walked quickly over to the table and returned with a surgical stapler and snapped four staples into the holy man's knee. This new pain was so great that Ellis passed out entirely as he had been doing more and more the last few days. A cup of alcohol was poured onto his treated wound before the priest's tormentor swiftly stepped back into the shroud of darkness.

After quickly changing into a clean suit, The Good Samaritan stepped outside into the warm night. The large door to the old building slid to a close and a thick padlock snapped the building secure. He stood there for a moment, taking a breath and realizing he was not alone. With a sigh of exasperation he turned to see a young woman standing at the bottom of the steps that lead to the main entrance.

It was Sarah Thompson. Time had not been kind to the young woman, now twenty four. She was thin, too thin, and looked like she'd be right at home in a soup kitchen somewhere. The Good Samaritan frowned at her presence, taking a moment to be disappointed in her growth into adulthood. She had a job, he had checked on that, and she had been set on the right path eight years earlier. He could tell she was malnourished but her natural beauty was still hiding beneath years of personal neglect. He shook his head and walked past her.

"There's nothing for you here," he said as he passed the desperate woman.

"There has to be," she said with sadness in her eyes, looking up at his massive height compared to hers. "There's nothing for me out there."

He ignored her and opened the door to a black sedan with silver trim and slid inside. Sarah walked up to the driver's side window and placed her hand on the glass. She hoped with her whole heart that he would just turn and look into her eyes.

Sarah pleaded with him through the glass, her muffled words just slipping through to his ears. "Just....please? I don't want anything from you. I just want to be here."

She jumped back as The Good Samaritan shifted the car into gear and sped through the dirt parking lot to the road, vanishing into the darkness. Sarah remained for a moment, silently begging for him to turn around.

There was a time when she would wait up at night, hoping that he would come to her window like Peter Pan came to Wendy. She used to play the scenario in her head; he would scoop her up and tell her that everything was going to be alright. With his deep, calm voice he would sooth her worries and take her away from whatever foster home she was in at the time.

Sarah looked around at the empty parking lot, then stared up at the looming building. Here she was again, just a scared little girl begging for attention from a person who would never offer it. Ashamed, she began the journey home. The nearest train station was twenty minutes away and the trains stopped running in fifteen minutes. Lots of time, she thought, to reflect on all the good decisions she had made that day.

———

The house was perfect. The gently winding roads snaked through the eye-catching properties, one after another, there were so many that it was hard to notice the four bedroom, two story home. At night it was hard to see because the neighborhood had switched to light pollution friendly alternatives years ago but the lawn was pristine. Inside, the home with dark hardwood floors was always kept clean. More than anything, it was quiet. Easily the most peaceful house on the block, it was rare the neighbors were even reminded that anyone lived there at all.

The dining room was equipped for elegant dinner parties that never happened. The beds were covered in exquisite sheets for visitors that never came. Every once in a while a neighbor paused to wonder just who the people were that occupied the home but little more was ever said about them. Some people, they thought, just aren't social and there's nothing wrong with that.

Headlights from a black sedan with silver trim flashed across the front windows, illuminating the white paint and wrap around porch. The door to the detached garage quietly opened as the vehicle pulled inside. The Good Samaritan stepped out of the car and approached his home as the garage door closed. He didn't often care much about his lawn, after all that was what he paid others to do, but as he approached the front door he took notice of the white tulips that had recently bloomed. Most people, he thought, were attracted to the colorful variety but he appreciated the simplicity of this flower.

The Good Samaritan unlocked his front door and entered the quiet home. The scent of a long stewing pot roast filled the air, the thermostat was set to a comfortable seventy three degrees and each lamp in each room emitted just enough light to reveal the room comfortably without any harsh or dim corners. From the kitchen came a pleasant voice.

"Hello, handsome."

Lily's bare feet walked down the hall towards the front door and she greeted her husband with a kiss. Lily was thirty four, sporting long blonde hair with a slight curl. She was an average height and beautiful but not in a distracting way. Her presence in any group or public setting was always regarded as pleasant and uneventful. The neighbors had been able to determine exactly these facts and nothing more about her, even less about her husband.

"How was work?" she asked as she took off his jacket and hung it on the coat rack near the door.

"Good," he replied without feeling the need to elaborate further.

She held his hand and led him towards the kitchen, "Come on, I tried something different this time. You're gonna love it."

She was right, the meal they had that night was above par and stood out as the best meal of the week. This was something that had become a bit of a routine, Lily competing with herself for that week's champion dinner. Her husband rarely offered a vote but occasionally she would catch a revealing "grunt" in the positive which she considered to be a firm support of that particular meal.

And so it was, every day, every week, every year. Clean, cook and wait. A master of keeping things in perspective, Lily looked around at her beautiful home and her strong, steady husband and knew that everything was just right. In fact, everything was perfect.

Chapter 4

Detective John Corbin shut the door to his apartment and locked the series of deadbolts and chains. He had always felt the number of locks was overkill but they had been there before him and he figured it was better to be safe than sorry, particularly considering the neighborhood he was in. It wasn't the worst part of town, he thought, but after the divorce he needed something and this place was affordable and near the station. Simple choice.

Corbin lived in a corner unit apartment that never allowed much sunlight due to the high rises on each side of the building. This meant that night was especially dark until the lights were on, something Corbin was reluctant to do given how easily he could see into the windows across the street and not wanting to join the "Rear Window Experience." The light over the stove was plenty to guide him through his living room where he tossed his keys on the coffee table and slumped onto the couch.

This day was exhausting, sure, but all days seemed to be. He laid down and stared at the ceiling, thinking about the days when he would come home and enjoy the company of a good woman. Corbin wasn't angry about the divorce, honestly it made sense. They had two kids and work came first, a story as simple as it was cliché. As a result, the judge made a lot of decisions that he couldn't argue with, including the choice to give nearly full custody to Rachel. The honest truth was that after Corbin moved out and got set up at his new "home" the kids would visit during the day every other weekend and not much about that was different than the way things had been before.

On the walls of the dimly lit corner apartment hung the basic set of single male decorating standards, but most of the photographs did remind him of better days. The facade of a whole family was alive and well in the flashes of moments displayed in each room. It felt forced, planting happy family photos, but in this way he was able to keep them close to him even though he had essentially chosen to keep them at distance. He felt that it was better to preserve his family as a memory rather than sacrifice the needs of the people he had sworn to protect in this city and he rarely second guessed this decision. In the end Rachel was a better parent than him and he knew that she was better off on her own, the kids needed a steady parenting presence.

As Corbin lay there it became clear that this would not be one of the nights that he eventually found himself sleeping in his bed. Passing out on the couch had become more and more common. As sleep overcame him he gladly accepted any rest that came without the extra effort of sleeping pills. Corbin had spent his time leaning on alcohol not only as emotional support but as a sleep aid and decided to leave it mostly behind. He had never really had an addictive personality but could see what a slippery slope that could be so after a period of depression he gave up what he considered to be "obligatory self-pity-based alcoholism." Every divorced man had to go through it, right?

Just as his eyes closed, Corbin felt a dark presence loom over him. Powerful hands reached out and wrapped around his throat. The detective tried to jump up to defend himself but his assailant was too strong, he tried to kick but his legs wouldn't move. He lay there, helpless, as the inhumanly powerful grip tightened.

Corbin looked up to make eye contact with his attacker. It was The Good Samaritan. Or was it? Truth be told, Corbin had never clearly seen his face, instead he relied only on the distorted security camera images that had been "enhanced." In fact, the man attacking him now was exactly this face he had seen so many times. Lacking any distinguishing features, the haunting face glaring down at him was grainy and distorted. What passed for eyes raged with anger and Corbin felt a fear that he had not felt since he was a child. His heart racing, the detective could feel fatigue setting in as his last attempts at breath begged to reach his lips.

Minutes passed. Corbin couldn't believe that he had survived this long and was overwhelmed by the crippling fear that refused to dissipate. Finally, he felt his last heartbeat and his muscles gave out. He woke up with a shudder. His clothes and the couch were now soaked with sweat, the room felt like it was a hundred degrees. He took a moment to check the room, obviously it was a dream but for some reason he had to know for sure.

He sat up. Perhaps, he thought, this would be a good night to sleep in his bed after all.

Chapter 5

Finding an affordable apartment had been challenging for Sarah. Waiting tables didn't exactly open up a lot of options so it was good that her standards were not particularly high. A few years back she found a roommate, Kelli, in this studio apartment which was crowded but it worked. Things had gotten more complicated when Kelli started bringing over a boyfriend and a strict "sex schedule" had to be created to allow for some privacy. When the happy couple decided to move in together Sarah was concerned about the tougher rent but relieved to know the studio would be all hers, men coming over for sex would no longer be an issue.

The space was cozy and suited her needs well, a welcome retreat from the rest of the world that she either hated or feared. It was rarely kept clean but if she were to have a visitor it would have been relatively simple to hide the least appealing areas (she had yet to invite a visitor to her home in all these years).

In the far corner a punching bag hung from the rafters above. The bag had been a gift from her foster father in home number three. Her experience in the system was stereotypical and abusive, but he had been the exception. He taught her to take care of her body and to protect herself which came in handy more than once after she aged out. The bag often found itself on the receiving end of Sarah's anger at the world around her. She had come to appreciate its presence as a friend in the apartment who would always be there to help her vent. This anthropomorphizing of an inanimate object made her worry about her own sanity from time to time. It didn't help that the bag was Wilson brand.

Sarah sat on her kitchen counter, her shoulder length hair lightly brushing her skin. The aforementioned boyfriend's parting gift to her was a Mets t-shirt he left under the couch. She couldn't care less about any sports but had to admit the oversized shirt was incredibly soft, she often sat by her kitchen window wearing only the shirt and found it quite peaceful. Although her bed had yet to play host to a male visitor, that's not to say she didn't enjoy a man's company every once in a while. But it was far from a priority. They served their purpose occasionally and then she was happy to move on.

The window glass had been cracked since Kelli had a spat with the neighbor across the alley and said neighbor retaliated by launching a beer bottle towards their apartment. In fairness, the loud music did stop after that so stirring that particular pot was effective. As Sarah stared out at the city the cracked glass streaked lines of warm street light across her face and down her body. There was an odd peacefulness to night time in the city, the noise and confusion all paused for a few hours so that those who caused all the commotion could rest and do it all over again in the morning.

She looked down at her arm and lifted the oversized sleeve to reveal the pit of her elbow. Track marks speckled her skin which had seen more than its fair share of needles. Heroin had been a staple for a few years now, Kelli had introduced her to the drug and had trouble seperating her habit from the rest of her life, but Sarah seemed to be able to keep it somewhat under control. She only ever used at home and only at night before bed, she didn't pretend she had cracked some sort of "heroin code" but at least she could sleep at night and function in the morning.

Sarah had learned the hard way to use the smaller gauge needles after month's of dealing with a nasty infection and no health insurance to help. She removed her needle and a small plastic bag from the wooden box sitting beside her. Sarah had a scented candle on the window sill which she preferred to use rather than a cigarette lighter which she always thought looked desperate. In her mind, by using the candle as her heat source this process was therapy, a lighter would mean that she was a drug addict.

After scooping the brown powder from the plastic bag Sarah patiently held it over the flame until it melted. She then carefully soaked the liquid into a piece of cotton and inserted the syringe, drawing back the drug into its vessel. She gently tied an old stocking around her arm and pulled tight, revealing her veins. She would have made a good nurse in a different life, finding the good vein was one of her hidden talents.

The needle slid into her skin and Sarah pushed the liquid into her vein. Immediately she felt the familiar rush of warmth and comfort as the tainted blood pumped through her system. She removed the tourniquet and relaxed against the cabinet, staring out at the street lights. A tear slid down her cheek as she admired the beauty of the halogen lamp piercing through the cracks in the glass.

These moments were important. A lifetime of wishing for better things carried a heavy weight and just a few hours of relief kept her in check. Without it, Sarah feared she would fall into the darkness of her own past and never escape. She sat up and leaned her head against the glass, her heart beat slowed and her eyelids grew heavier.

On the street three stories below, two men pushed someone into the alley. They slammed him up against the wall and began shouting with hushed voices. Sarah watched, barely able to react to the violence but inhaled deeply.

The attackers began to beat the man until he fell to the ground where they decided he needed a little more convincing.

Sarah slowly placed her hand on the window and lightly tapped it in a sluggish attempt to gain their attention. Satisfied with their assault, the men took their victim's wallet and slipped off his shoes before running away from the scene. Sarah silently begged for the beaten man to begin moving which he never did. She turned and fumbled for her phone like a toddler trying to hold chopsticks and it fell to the floor. For a moment she considered engaging in the exhausting task of lowering herself to the floor and picking up her phone to call the police but sleep took her before she could muster the energy.

Sarah slid back into the cabinet with a thump and drifted into a deep sleep. She would regret this sleeping position the next morning and likely much more when she looked down on the alley in the light of day.

———————

The thick air that hung in the warehouse main floor had finally begun to cool now that the tremendous heat of the sun had gone for the night. Father Ellis remained bound to the thick wooden chair at the center of the floor, attempting to enjoy the rest from his torture.

He never heard voices or even so much as a vehicle outside. He thought it could be that the man who held him captive had so effectively sound proofed the building that truly no sounds at all could enter or escape. But it was also possible that this place was so desperately isolated that there were, in fact, no other souls in the area at all. The idea that his solitude was so much worse than immediately evident added a weight of desperation to his heart. Being stranded alone in the room was a nightmare, but what if there were no one around for miles?

In the evenings, when the stranger went to whatever keeps a murderer busy at night, Father Ellis found himself alone with his thoughts. Sleep would come intermittently. It was impossible to stay awake after such exhaustive torment but it was equally impossible to find himself comfortable enough to actually sleep. Each time he awoke, after studying the room and confirming that he was still alone, he found himself looking inward at the wretch of a man he had become.

There was a time, he thought, that he was in love with the church and had a pure relationship with Christ. Not all of that had changed but the devil had infected his mind and forced him to do unspeakable things. Now he was sure that he was condemned to hell and that a lifetime of servitude in the church was the only salvation, but the urges never left him.

Lisa Harper. A tear ran down his bloody cheek as he remembered the sounds of her screams before she became numb to their time behind locked doors. The shame was unbearable and he found himself longing for the twisted tools he had been subjected to for the last several days. Again he pictured the innocent girl in his office, her clothes on the floor, and he turned to the table of weapons with desperation hoping that one would jump towards him and punish him as he deserved.

Ellis' heart raced as a panic attack set in, the physical exhaustion pushed him over the edge and he passed out for no more than a few moments. When he awoke he surveyed the room, not knowing how much time had passed. After reassuring himself that he was alone, he took a deep breath and calmed his mind. Slowly, memories of his crimes slipped back into his mind and he once again yearned for the sweet release of excruciating pain.

Chapter 6

The millennial renaissance of boutique coffee houses had come in waves a few years prior and after the initial rush it was only the strong that survived. The Good Samaritan and his wife sat in surprisingly comfortable chairs outside The Mean Bean which had become Lily's favorite some time ago. She held her iced caramel macchiato with both hands, deeply engaged in a one way conversation with her husband who hadn't yet touched his black drip coffee. She never understood his coffee preferences; drinking drip coffee at all, much less black, seemed like the modern day equivalent of a flagellant whipping themselves in penance.

"... and so I told her that I'm not going to spend my whole day cleaning up after her mistakes." Lily had the spectacular ability to talk for hours at a time without receiving a single response.

The Good Samaritan engaged with her in eye contact occasionally but spent most of this time observing the people who passed by on the sidewalk beside them. Public places downtown were a virtual fish tank of sinners and evil doers. It just took a cunning eye to spot them.

"And of course, Judy doesn't see any of this, so she thinks that Carol's doing a bang up job and that I'm just another one of her helpers."

A woman passed by, dressed in the latest of fabletics. Unmarried but seemingly content with life as it seemed to be at the moment.

"I'm telling you, sweetie, you are so lucky you don't have to deal with all of this gossipy crap."

In the opposite direction, a man hurried past. He was late but not for work. Dressed in jeans and a button down, he was on his way to a friend's house. A good man? Perhaps but not entirely. Just behind him a teenage girl struggled behind the force of two large dogs. A part time job. An innocent.

"I can't believe how freakin' hot it is out here. It's April for God's sake."

From inside The Mean Bean a couple left holding two identical drink orders, both very fit and dressed to show it. Neither seemed to acknowledge the other as they approached their vehicle and got in. Troubled, certainly, but nothing sinister. A female voice could be heard shouting from behind closed windows in the vehicle parked behind the couple. The Good Samaritan glanced over his shoulder, a business woman who earned her way to the top but arrived there honestly.

"You know it's the hottest it's been in like forty years or something?"

From around the corner ahead of The Good Samaritan a man appeared with a casual walk. A familiar face. The patient observer tilted his head slightly as if to confirm what he knew to be true. This man was indeed familiar. It had been a few years but he was once a resident of the chair set in the middle of a warehouse lost in the abyss of a forgotten part of town.

"Christopher.." The Good Samaritan whispered to himself.

Shocked by the sudden contribution to the conversation, Lily stopped and turned to her husband. "What was that?"

Before The Good Samaritan could answer, Christopher recognized the man he was unknowingly approaching. His eyes widened and his heart stopped.

On instinct Christopher immediately turned and bolted in the opposite direction, not noticing the cafe table in his way which caught his lower half. Christopher toppled into the sidewalk face first which tore a gash over his right eyebrow but he quickly shot back up and continued his escape.

The commotion caught the attention of everyone enjoying the warm breeze outside The Mean Bean. Lily turned to The Good Samaritan, "What the hell was that?"

He simply shook his head, seemingly unphased by the sudden change in atmosphere and sat back in his chair. Then he stood and buttoned his coat, "I'm going to step inside for a moment."

Lily nodded and returned to her sugary drink, her eyebrows still raised in surprise by Christopher's dramatic display. As The Good Samaritan passed through the coffee shop and out the back door he reflected on the time he had spent with his prey.

Christopher Rivera was an obese slob but that was not his sin, at least not the sin The Good Samaritan was concerned with. He had spent most of his adult life in the securities industry until he eventually ran his own investment firm that did quite well. While greedy hedge fund managers are nothing too unique, Rivera managed to stay below the radar for quite some time by keeping his appetite small and only targeting middle class families. In the end, he had stolen over seven hundred million dollars and went completely unnoticed by the SEC. A staggering number of families lost everything in the scandal.

Knowing the secrets of the city is helpful when hunting degenerates. As Christopher swung around a corner two blocks away, now drenched in sweat and limping with a muscle cramp, The Good Samaritan was already waiting for him. He slammed the obese man into the wall of a barber shop that closed years before and he collapsed to the ground in tears.

"No!" he pleaded, "I'm sorry!"

The Good Samaritan grabbed him by the ankle and dragged him into the nearby alley with surprising ease considering the man's mass. After a dozen feet the two men were mostly hidden by the shadows of the morning sun. The Good Samaritan knelt down, grabbed his hair and pushed Christpohers head into the red brick.

"I'm sorry, ok?" Christopher was forcing his words through tears and gasps for breath, squinting his right eye to keep the blood out of it, "Listen I just got scared, I was a little freaked out, that's all. Look, I swear, I gave it all up. I got an honest job now, I-I'm working for the city, doin' the trash pick-up."

Over the years The Good Samaritan learned that eyes told more truth than any words ever could. He searched Christophers quivering face for signs of deceit.

"I gave it all up. I gave it all up, I swear! I just didn't expect to see you and I freaked out, that's all, I swear! See?" Christopher had reached into his pocket and pulled out a key card name tag that granted him access to the Solid Waste Disposal Complex.

The Good Samaritan briefly studied the ID then nodded as he released his grip on Christpher's hair. He stood dominant over the former wall street king and left the alley as he adjusted his shirt and coat back to perfect symmetry. A moment later he settled back into his chair across from Lily who smiled at his return.

His bitter coffee still hot, The Good Samaritan finally took his first sip as he continued to study the pedestrians on the sidewalk.

Chapter 7

Warren Shefflied walked through the doors of the twenty third precinct with pride. He carried himself like a man of honor despite having very little to speak of. He walked with a purpose, having spent the last thirty minutes in his car preparing himself. Warren was middle aged, overweight and just above average height. He was hard to look at but impossible to ignore as there wasn't a visible square inch on his body that wasn't scarred. His sandy blonde hair was falling out of place and he carelessly brushed it with his fingers as he pushed through the doors to the squad room.

Detective John Corbin was sitting at his desk, studying the case file for a recent domestic dispute gone bad. The Good Samaritan case had consumed so much of his life the last few years that these other cases seemed so simple by comparison. There weren't years of history to trace, no morally ambiguous motives, no dead bodies cleaned of any physical evidence with surgical precision. Just a drunk asshole and a woman who should have left long ago.

Corbin saw a large man with a limp approach one of the deputies who pointed in his direction. Warren approached his desk and stood for a moment before speaking, Corbin continued reading his report until spoken to.

"I was told you were the man to see." Warren said with sweat beading on his forehead.

"Oh yeah?" Corbin still had not looked up to see the man's face. "About what?

This was it. The moment Warren had been preparing for and feared for so long. He took a deep breath. "About a man who kidnaps people in the middle of the night, tortures them, degrades them, and then plays judge and jury with their life."

Corbin swiveled in his chair and looked up at Warren, scanning him from his feet to his sweaty forehead. "Who are you?"

Warren's lips tightened and he took another deep breath, "I'm the one that got away."

Corbin figured this day would come but so much time had passed that he began to think it impossible. He had interviewed the surviving family members of dead bodies that had been dumped, he had interviewed criminals that had been tortured and released to the custody of the police. But this was the first time a man walking the streets in freedom had chosen to volunteer any information.

Within just a few minutes the two men sat in an interview room, cameras and audio recorders rolling. Waren stared at his hands that he could no longer feel after extensive nerve damage. The detective was reciting some required speech about his rights and the conversation being recorded but all Warren could hear was that deep, inhuman voice in his head.

> *"You need to understand what just happened here, because it doesn't happen very often. I was told that you should be allowed to live and to do so in the comfort of your home instead of a prison where you belong. You have been granted an opportunity to start fresh, begin a new life. You can be a decent man now. You must*

never tell anyone that you were here. I will be watching you and I will know if you do. I have a whole graveyard full of people that thought it was over, and then returned to sin. You will be grateful for your time here. You will be, or you will die."

Warren swallowed and shivered in his chair. Corbin started easy, establishing dates and circumstances. Waren shared the same physical description he had heard many times. It was plain to see that this man had been through an incredible amount of pain and quite evident how terrified he was. As they spoke his eyes continued to check the corners as if it were possible some apparition might suddenly appear.

"So you know I need to ask" said Corbin, knowing what the response would be, "what did you do? I mean, assuming you're not the one person who was completely innocent."

Warren nodded, "No, I'm not. I wasn't. But I'm not like, under oath, right?"

"That's correct. You don't have to answer."

"Ok then," Warren sighed in relief, "yeah I just, let's say it was a hard time. It's over now and I'm done with all that. The problem now is just trying to live. You know, you go to prison and you can pretty much get out and rejoin the world for the most part. But with this guy, you don't...nothing is ever the same."

Corbin had been craving inside information on this man's crimes for years, but something about this interview was already striking a nerve. The silent impudence of a criminal hiding behind this testimony was surely something he wasn't interested in but he allowed it to continue.

"For a while I didn't want to be seen in public." Warren admitted. "Wouldn't even leave the house, lookin' the way I do. I can still feel their eyes on me. Every person in every room...curious. They don't want to look, but they can't help but wonder... 'How did he get like that?' And who could blame them?"

Warren checked the corner again before continuing, "You know, what sort of thing would a man go through to wind up looking like that? Who did that to him? Why?"

"I suppose the 'why?' is the hardest part." Corbin explored.

Warren looked up at the detective's eyes, "Yeah. I-yeah I guess it is."

Corbin allowed for a moment of silence to drift by. It was time to learn some hard facts from the first person he had ever spoken to personally who could offer them. He had great respect for the previous detectives who had been assigned the case but he knew with a little concrete direction he could make some progress. This psychopath had been so effective at traumatizing his victims that they absolutely never came forward like this. At some point it would be prudent to learn why Warren was the exception but Corbin wasn't about to question this gift as it was being offered to him.

"Ok," Corbin sat forward, "tell me what happened."

Warren had this part of his statement rehearsed but suddenly the words weren't coming as easily as he had planned. He sat back and looked straight ahead, not really at Corbin but beyond him as if staring at his own memory.

"He tied me to a chair for twelve days," Warren recalled. "That...chair. God, that fucking chair. It's...in my head, I can't get it out. The chair scared me as much as he did. It had God knows how many people's blood on it. He sliced me up, beat me up. Every day, something new. It was like he was trying new things for sport. Pipes, knives, fire, water. Anything he could think of."

Corbin wrote quickly as Warren continued, "Then he told me, it was time to decide whether I would live or die. I was ready to be judged...and sentenced."

This was the problem, Corbin thought, with the vigilante element. He was not the most popular cop in town as a result of his pursuit of this case. When the killings first began it was easy to want this him behind bars but as more and more victim's piled up the line between right and wrong became very blurry. Most cops couldn't handle the idea of standing up for the rights of rapists and murderers. It was a hard stand to take but rights are rights no matter what piece of trash is claiming them. Whatever Warren did was condemnable, he was sure of that, but he deserved a fair trial. Everyone does.

"Then it got real quiet." Warren said, seemingly pausing for dramatic effect. "He told me that I'd been given a second chance at life, that I would eventually be grateful for this experience."

Warren's voice began to break as he said those words out loud. *Grateful* was not a word he was comfortable with. "And he let me go. So, here I am."

"Have you heard from him since?" asked Corbin.

"No. But I see him everywhere. He's stalking me, just like he promised he would. I'll check behind me and catch him through a window. Take out my trash and see that shadow. He doesn't try to hide. He wants me to know he's there."

"Well, then it will be easy to find him." Corbin said with sincere confidence.

"Not really. He doesn't keep to any routine, I never know when he's going to show up. And now that I've come to you, by tomorrow, I'll either be dead or back in that chair."

"We can protect you," Corbin shot back.

Warren nodded, "Yeah, for how long?"

"It depends on how helpful you wind up being," Corbin explained, "So far, you haven't told me anything that can help me catch this guy."

Warren thought for a moment. He knew things no one in the police department knew, even if he had been kept in the dark about almost everything, there were some things that couldn't be hidden.

"How about a face? And I'll bet there's only so many warehouses that look like that in this city. He doesn't know it but I saw it from the outside when he was bringing me in"

Optimism wasn't John Corbin's finest quality but it was hard to resist a modest smile.

Chapter 8

The yellow cab pulled up to the intimidating warehouse, the driver looking around nervously. Sitting in his back seat was a young girl, only fourteen or fifteen, and she had asked to be taken here. This whole section of town was nearly pitch black as if the mayor of this particular hell hole had forgotten to pay the electric bill. The vehicle came to a stop and the driver turned to the teenager.

"Miss, I can't leave you here. No way," pleaded the driver.

"It's ok," she said with confidence, "my dad works here and sometimes he works late. I always take a cab and the other drivers are always worried too. I'll be ok."

Her well rehearsed speech out of the way, she paid the man in cash and slid out the back seat, slinging her backpack over her shoulder as she slammed the door. The driver watched her walk away for twenty feet before shaking his head and pulling away.

Lisa Harper approached the broad wooden steps that led to the powerful looking front doors. Putting on a brave face to minimize questions for the cab driver was easy, suddenly her knees felt weak as she cautiously took the first step. There were only six steps but they felt like a mountain as she pushed herself forward and upwards. Once at the door she raised her fist to knock on the door. She filled her lungs with air and swung her fist forward with her eyes closed. Nothing.

She opened her eyes to see that the entryway was already open. Standing just within the shadows, The Good Samaritan held the large door ajar and gestured for her to come inside. Suddenly her knees were no longer weak. As she stepped inside she studied her own feelings, shocked at the dramatic shift. Here she was, in easily the most terrifying place she had ever been, being escorted by a man with a massive and dark presence who had killed God knows how many people. He was a murderer, simply put. And she felt safe.

Lisa was led into a small room by her escort. The room was charmingly comfortable. On the way there she passed empty hallways and abandoned rooms covered in dust and dirt. There was no decor of any kind, except for a large collection of old mattresses, they lined the walls within the rooms and could be found scattered throughout the building. The floorboards creaked as they crossed them, embracing the true audio and visual experience of a haunted house. All of this and then she found herself in a room that truly made an effort to be accommodating to guests.

There was a couch, old and worn but comfortable nevertheless. She sat and looked around at the small efforts to decorate, an old lamp, a fairly new looking rug. In a place that was clearly designed to elicit fear, this room was practically a day spa.

"Thank you for coming," The Good Samaritan finally spoke.

She nodded as he stepped forward and stood over her. "This won't be easy. But it must be done. This man that you trusted; Ellis. I've seen every kind of evil in this world. He is truly evil. What happened to you was wrong and I have seen to his punishment. He is truly repentant. Of that I am sure. But what happens to him now is not my choice. The choice is yours. I will take you to see him now and if you wish it, I will put him down. If you should choose mercy, I will see to it that he is delivered to the police at which point I can no longer control his fate. Do you understand?"

A moment later they pushed through another large set of doors that led into a massive interior room. Lisa gasped at the space that didn't seem possible from the outside. The walls were lined with more mattresses and old machinery was stacked high forming a loose ring around the center of the room which had just one large light hanging from the ceiling. As The Good Samaritan led her past the derelict machines, the center of the floor was revealed.

There was Father Ellis, whom she had known since she had been in the second grade, he had been strapped to a dark red chair just beneath the large light. On the floor all around him for at least ten feet out was a dark stain that was much darker than the rest of the floor. The man himself had been stripped naked and was slumped over, his hands bound behind the chair. Father Ellis had always been an oddly shaped man, thin in every way except for a bit of a pot belly that made him look like a lowercase "b". And of course this wasn't her first time seeing him naked but seeing him in this state was especially pathetic.

He was beaten nearly beyond recognition. Lisa tried to find a part of his body that hadn't yet been injured, dried blood coated his skin and she could see that several bones were broken including most of his fingers and his ankle which twisted in a direction that was unnatural. Her first step in his direction sounded like a cannon as she approached him.

Lisa's mind raced. She was no killer, how could she be expected to have this man put to death? In truth, she saw herself as a good Christian and there is certainly no gray area in being a willing accessory to murder is acceptable. She was young but she had grown up quickly and some of these things were easy to know. No, she decided, she would not be the one to put this man to death. That was up to the police.

As she got closer, the smell began to reach her. At first she noticed a putrid stench of a man who had been sweating for a week without bathing, then came the faded scent of burnt flesh, and lastly came a familiar smell. She recognized it immediately but couldn't quite identify it. Perfume. It was the perfume that Father Ellis sprayed on himself every morning.

She had first noticed the flowery scent the day that Ellis invited her to stay late after bible study when she was ten years old. He had never been that close to her before and it was the first thing that made her realize something unusual was happening. Ellis had insisted on being the one to take Lisa home that day and continued to chauffeur her for years after. Lisa took a sharp breath at the thought of the day she first became unclean. Father Ellis was careful to remind her that her sins could be forgiven as he cried tears of shame, his naked body standing over her. Nothing was ever the same after that, the difference between right and wrong was nearly impossible to distinguish.

She spent the next five years in an endless loop of shame and absolution. Father Ellis would take her into his study where she would sin and the next day she would be forgiven. She knew that he had a heavy burden to bear as the leader of the church and even men of God sometimes have weaknesses. He reminded her every day that if she wanted to be there for her family and for the church, she needed to help him be strong and rid him of his vices. She knew no one would understand such a complicated set of circumstances so she hid the truth from her parents and everyone she trusted. It wasn't until The Good Samaritan approached her that she even realized something was wrong and from there it was a sharp decline of shame.

Once her eyes were opened to the reality of what had been done to her she couldn't eat for days and never slept. Lisa went through rapid fire stages of anger, shame and depression until the day that Father Ellis was abducted. She hated herself for being so stupid to let it happen but was quickly learning to hate this villain far more.

She finally reached the beacon of light that shone down on her rapist. She glared at him with rage-filled eyes that had been almost sympathetic when she first walked into the room. Ellis noticed her presence and tried to lift his head, looking at her with his one good eye. He attempted to speak but only guttural whispers came out.

Lisa's lip quivered and her fists clenched so hard she could feel her nails piercing into her skin. She snapped around and walked away from Ellis who watched her exit the light. He saw her pause for a moment beside the monstrous man who had been punishing him for his sins, she whispered something and then she quickly left. The Good Samaritan slowly approached the center of the room with his hands behind his back and bent at the hip to whisper in Father Ellis' ear.

"Your wicked time on this Earth has come to an end," he whispered with a haunting calmness.

The Good Samaritan stood straight and began to walk away as Father Ellis' pulse quickened. Step after step, the distance between them grew as Ellis used what little strength he had left to try to escape his bonds. Then The Good Samaritan turned.

Lisa reached the front doors and jumped at the sound of a gunshot slamming through the hallways. Without turning back, she opened the door and stepped back into the light.

As Sarah walked down the sidewalk she removed her work uniform shirt to reveal a white tank top underneath. She slung the sweaty Tap Seventeen uniform shirt over her shoulder and enjoyed what little breeze now touched her pale skin. These walks had become tradition for her on the rare days that she left work while it was still daylight. The sun was just beginning to set now so that the asphalt and rooftops could have a chance to cool down for a few hours before the cycle repeated the next day.

She took a seat on the short wall surrounding Fulton Park and crossed her legs. The park, perfectly lovely during the day as it was filled with moms and nannies, would be clearing out soon to allow for the night time crowd which was considerably less family friendly. Sarah never understood the habit of doing drugs in social groups and traveling to a city park of all places to do them. The comfort and privacy of her own home was her preference, plus it's considerably less likely you'll be arrested there.

Her perch on the stone wall gave her a good view of several small storefronts that lined the street opposite Fulton Park. She did like her neighborhood despite its shortcomings and lack of curb appeal. Sarah didn't see the age and grime, she saw character and authenticity. There wasn't a Starbucks anywhere in this zip code, even McDonalds stayed away for fear of robberies. No, these businesses were privately owned and privately protected. She knew the whole block was ripe for gentrification but was glad that, for now, the old charm still thrived.

But of course the charm had its pitfalls. Sarah chose this particular spot today for a reason. She lit a cigarette and waited patiently. The silent observer listened for the door chime of the Lucky Saver to ring across the street. The Saver was owned by an Armenian family that had been there longer than most of the other businesses, selling the daily essentials of milk, candy bars and scratch off lottery tickets. She had never learned their names but the grandfather owned the shop and ran the day time operations, his son took over at night with the other kids and grandkids splitting the other responsibilities around their school schedules. It was the American Dream, she thought, a family moving here and making it work with only each other to rely on. Sarah had always found it quite humbling.

She waited for forty seven minutes until the sun had fully set and the street lights came on. It was hard to predict when they would come. Eventually, after an assortment of innocent shoppers had come and gone from the Lucky Saver, she heard the bell ring and turned to see what she had been waiting for. Two young men entered the shop and pretended to be customers for a brief moment before one pointed a revolver at the old man while the second kept watch. It was a shake down, one that had become routine and increasingly violent.

Sarah snuffed out her current cigarette and pulled out her phone to jot down the time and number of assailants including their description. The time caught her attention and she looked up. It was almost time for the son to take over and she hoped he would be just a minute late. If he were to walk in on the robbery in progress things could go bad quickly. The grandfather calmly prepared the cash in the register as he had done before. Sarah had seen this occur two other times.

Upon being handed the wad of cash the thug shouted something at the old man before swinging the pistol and striking him in the head. The two men left the shop in less of a hurry than they went in and casually walked down the street, walking with the confidence of men who knew no one would call the police. Sarah seethed as they rounded the corner and she jumped off the wall in pursuit.

She kept her distance, careful to stay in the shadows should one of them turn around. At this point and at this hour she was less concerned that they would know she witnessed their crime and more concerned about being a woman alone on a dark street. Sarah didn't have to follow them for very long as they stepped into an apartment building just two blocks away. In fact, this building was only three blocks away from her own.

The old brick building was "U" shaped and the apartments all had exterior facing doors. Sarah positioned herself beneath a tree near the front gate and watched the men ascend to the seventh floor and enter unit number "7C". She notated the address and number in her phone and proceeded down the street.

She chuckled at herself for her musings earlier. *The American Dream.*

"Land of opportunity," she said to no one and she turned the corner to go home and feel a little bit better about the world with the help of a needle.

Chapter 9

The hallways of precinct twenty three were severely outdated, they screamed eighties cop movie and it bothered John Corbin every time he walked through them. Modern conveniences had been peppered here and there but the look and feel was largely "retro", which he did not approve of. Corbin was beginning his day today with a newfound sense of optimism, Warren had agreed to give an official statement which would then be prepared for release to the press. Before then, however, it was time to try their luck with the sketch artist.

Sketches of The Good Samaritan did exist but they were rare and Corbin himself had never had the opportunity to walk a witness through the process. He reminded himself that Warren's statement was a far cry from a breakthrough in the case but it was the closest thing to progress he had seen in months so it was worth getting just a little excited over.

"Corbin," the calm voice came from within the Captain's office as the detective walked by.

"Sir?" Corbin replied, knowing that this sort of interaction was rarely a positive one. He stepped just beyond the threshold of Captain Morton's doorway. Morton was an interesting shape, having let himself go after years of not being on the street but he was built like a linebacker so even today his shoulders and chest looked ready for a fight as they rested above a belly that had seen a few too many cheesesteaks. Morton had liked Corbin at first, glad to see a fellow black man rise in the ranks, but their relationship quickly soured.

"I was just talking to Jackson," Morton said with the tone of a teacher about to scold a student caught cheating.

"Yeah?" Corbin responded, making a mental note to tell Jackson to mind his own damn business next time.

"He told me something that upset me very much," he was still speaking in that calm-before-the-storm voice, "and I wanted to talk to you before I overreacted. You know how I do that, don't you John?"

"Yes, sir." *Shit.*

"He told me that you spent your whole day on this serial killer case. Now I assumed that he was exaggerating, of course you wouldn't be wasting your time on a case that I told you specifically not to pursue."

That was true. It had been 'suggested' that he drop the case no less than seven times but that never seemed to quite sink in. The Captain continued, "But then I saw that you got a witness in there with Simon. Now, what case is that man a witness in?"

Corbin looked out into the bullpen where his new friend Warren was sitting with Simon, the sketch artist. Simon worked diligently as Warren dictated, gently marking the sketchpad as he continued. Old school sketching was something that Corbin was glad to still have around, the computer software always lacked personality and allowing a little emotional association was sometimes helpful when searching for a suspect.

"Corbin!" the Captain was losing his patience "What case is that man a witness in?"

"The um, serial killer case, sir." Corbin managed to maintain eye contact for that sentence which surprised him.

"Uh-huh. Why?"

This was an opportunity, "This guy's not scared, Captain. He wants to make it public. He's gonna take it to the media and we'll have the whole goddamn city looking for this guy."

Morton contained his rage with every ounce of energy he had, "I am sick of hearing about this. I am sick of you wasting taxpayers money on a guy that kills people that no one likes."

Corbin had always struggled with this, he couldn't wrap his head around the concept that a psychopath deserved a free pass for crimes of this nature. A vigilante is still a criminal and the law doesn't get to pick and choose. Other detectives had turned down the case time and time again out of a distaste for the idea of having to defend the rights of murderers and rapists.

Morton continued, "I am sick of looking over at your desk and seeing a pile of folders for cases that I gave you three weeks ago. You cannot ignore your other cases. Every one of those folders has got a wife or husband or brother or sister or whatever attached to it and they want justice too. Now, I get why you want to catch him so bad and if you do, I'll be glad. But you have three weeks to wrap this shit up or you will be cleaning out your desk, is that clear?"

"Three weeks?" Corbin protested, scoffing at the idea a case more than a decade old could suddenly be solved within such a time frame. But he did have a point, Corbin thought, there were a number of other cases waiting for his attention. He tried to address them as often as possible but even he had to admit that focusing on The Good Samaritan case came at a price.

Corbin turned to leave but Morton called after him, "And Corbin."

The detective turned. Suddenly the Captain was no longer speaking in a nice, calm voice. "If Simon shows me one more sketch of a blonde hair, blue eyed, Arian Nation looking mother-fucker like all the other ones you got on your desk, I will personally take each and every one and stuff them up your ass with a fucking broom stick!"

The hustle of the squad room came to an absolute silence as all looked in their direction. Corbin turned to see Jackson with his jaw dropped and suppressing a smile, a deputy to his right unable to contain a chuckle and even Warren had turned with a look of bewilderment. Detective John Corbin left his Captain's office and stepped into the bullpen to begin the final few weeks of this case.

Chapter 10

The downtown city sidewalk was home to thousands of innocent and evil people every day, there were few other places that one could go to take in such a selection. The Good Samaritan took his time, walking slowly in between the storefront windows and parking meters, surrounded by the morning horde of bustling humans.

This was his shopping mall, he sometimes felt like a kid choosing his ice cream flavor out of all the options. As he stepped through the crowd he studied each and every face, never knowing what exactly he was looking for. There was a feeling that would come when someone was hiding a darkness. No one could ever truly hide evil, he had confirmed, not from him. In truth, most people knew when someone was a bad person but lacked the courage or placed too much faith in the American judicial system to do anything about it.

All of these people, he thought, had it within them to destroy lives. If he had proven anything to himself over the years it was that he could find them and know their secrets. In the distance he caught a glimpse through the sea of shoulders and hair. A face. She pushed her way through the crowd towards The Good Samaritan and something in her eyes betrayed her. He stopped, allowing the mass of pedestrians to flow past him like water moves around a river rock.

The Good Samaritan studied her face as time slowed all around him. He was never able to see her for more than a second or two as others would obstruct his view in their hurry to work. As the woman got closer he learned more. She sported blonde hair that was gray at the roots, a black pantsuit that was masculine in its design. Her eyes were a dark brown which did not compliment her light hair well and the lines on her face made her seem older than she likely was. There seemed to be evidence of a permanent frown that had taken a toll on her skin. Otherwise, she was very fit and The Good Samaritan guessed she had worked out this morning as she did most mornings before work.

She did not look up to make eye contact with anyone on the street. A crowded city can be remarkably private, but she seemed to be making a distinct effort to avoid connection. A small twitch in the corner of her lip told him that something was heavy on her mind today in particular. She was clearly a woman in the corporate world and that could lead to all kinds of stress which would easily explain many of these signs. But this was different, something caught his eye from the beginning and he decided it was time to pursue further information.

The woman slipped past him, her shoulder lightly brushing his. He took in her scent as she passed. Once she had taken a few steps away from him, The Good Samaritan turned and began his pursuit. This was a process and they were only on the first step. Before anything, he needed to learn her name and where she worked. From there he could access nearly any information he could possibly want, including whatever she was hiding from the world.

Sloane Kelli worked for one of the largest advertising agencies in the country having been personally responsible for several international rebrands. She had broken the glass ceiling only recently when she became the first female VP at Franklin Global. Her position as an account executive for the better part of the last decade was not a creative position but certainly an important one as she was responsible for the execution and world wide distribution of multiple accounts.

In truth, she should have been made VP years earlier but sexism in the workplace was a difficult maze to navigate: fight too hard and you turn off your male superiors, too little and you get ignored. Having achieved her position was no small feat and she told herself that every day. She maintained her upward progression with a carefully fine tuned routine that started with a 4:30 alarm in the morning followed by a minimal breakfast and an hour at the gym. She arrived at work by 7:45 every day, sometimes beating even the security guards. Sloane never left before 7pm and usually stayed later depending on client needs that day.

She never took vacations but was recently sent on an upstate trip for a client meeting and she chose to look at it as a getaway. The morning of the meeting she even slept in until 5:30 before heading to the hotel gym. That evening she chose to drive home rather than stay another night and began the trip home on the poorly lit mountain roads.

In fairness, it wasn't her fault. The client had insisted on a toast after they had negotiated the contract and wine was poured. The second glass was also forced upon her and it felt rude to refuse as the bottle was quite expensive. It was less than an hour later that she found herself staring down at the broken body of a cyclist.

He had been driving on the proper side of the road just after sunset, there were multiple electric lights on his cycle and helmet. She struggled to imagine how she hadn't seen him but the left turn was so sharp. Sloane had done her best to hug the lines on the endlessly curving road which had been going well as there were seemingly no other cars on the road. On this turn, however, she swung wide right just as the cyclist revealed himself around the bend and the headlights flashed against his bright yellow jersey.

She waited for what felt like an eternity, stopped on the side of the road, for the man to move. Eventually it was clear he wasn't getting up on his own so she slowly exited her car and crept around to the hood. There she saw a collage of red and yellow draped over a heap of torn flesh and broken bone. She hadn't just hit the man, he had fallen under the wheel and been tossed out the passenger side of the car where he was now pinned up against the metal barrier just before the steep slope. His arm was pushed between the spokes of the front bicycle wheel, his head slid underneath the barrier and was turned further than his spine should have allowed.

Sloane Kelli thought quickly and attempted to remain standing as she fought the effects of her heightened heart rate and rapid breaths. She did the math, two glasses of wine with such generous pours had to be at least a point oh nine blood alcohol level. There was no version of this story where she didn't wind up with at the very least a DUI which would derail her career by itself, nevermind a vehicular manslaughter charge.

Everything she had built was burning right before her eyes. She quickly developed a list of options in her head, first turning to look at the front of her car, it was barely damaged. Sloane scanned the road once more, confirming that the two of them were entirely alone. She peered over the edge of the railing at the steep drop to the forest below. There was no list of options, the answer was cold blooded but clear. One life had already ended due to this tragic incident, there was no reason to destroy two lives.

Sloane Kelli used to worry about doing too much strength training for fear that it would make her arms appear overly masculine. In his moment, she was thankful for her ability to deadlift a fully grown man just enough to roll his body over the railing. The corpse slid down the short rock cliff and then fell to the brush below with a disturbing crunch. Her whole body began to shake as the reality of what she was doing set in, then she lifted the bike and tossed it over the side, careful not to let it strike the body.

It was done. She didn't allow herself to stare much longer as she scanned the environment for anything else that needed to be disposed of. A few plastic pieces from the bike had to be collected but the bigger problem was the sizable pile of blood that had gathered underneath the railing. Sloane turned and reached into her car for a water bottle and squeezed its contents toward the blood, once it was empty the deep red had diluted enough that it was unlikely anyone would notice it from the road.

Sloane turned to her vehicle and quickly slid into the driver's seat. She put her hands on the wheel, realizing for the first time that they were covered in blood. She vowed to solve that problem at a later time as she shifted the car into drive and sped off.

Sloane had come home covered in blood and therefore had to tell the story to her husband but had otherwise successfully hidden the tragedy and returned to a relatively normal life. He was a coward and she would have preferred to hide it from him as well which would have been easy if not for the incriminating stains. Only seven days had passed when she brushed the shoulder of the mysterious stranger on the city sidewalk. Two days later she was leaving the office for the day at 8:35 p.m., the last one to head home for the day. After keeping a close eye on the news reports she learned that the body had been found but there seemed to be no way to connect her to the accident. She reached her hand out to open the lobby doors that lead to the street.

"County road four eighty six," said a chilling voice from the shadows. The words made her blood turn to ice and she slowly turned to find the source. The Good Samaritan stepped into the light.

"Who are you?" she begged.

The strange man pulled a small digital audio recorder out of his pocket and pressed play. After a few seconds Sloane heard a familiar voice.

"I'm sorry, I don't know what you're talking about," the nervous voice said.

"Richard?" Sloane whispered as she recognized her husband's voice.

"I-I mean, I heard about the guy getting killed on the news, but Sloane didn't have anything to do with it," an unseen force caused Richard to wince in pain. *"Oh, Jesus. What ... what do you want?"*

Sloane stepped closer to hear her husband's desperate voice, unconsciously stepping closer to the terrifying man.

"Oh, God. Please don't kill me, please don't kill me. Look she was there, but it wasn't her fault, okay? She hit him with her car, but he got right back up, he said he was fine."

Suddenly the voice screamed out in pain, a tear escaped Sloane's eye.

"He died right there! She had had a couple of drinks so she freaked. She rolled his body out of the road and took off. Oh, god..." Richard desperately confessed.

A loud thud was heard on the recording before The Good Samaritan turned it off and returned it to his pocket. Richard Kelli had been technically innocent and was therefore left with a lenient bruise with which to remember the encounter. The Good Samaritan had found the man pathetic and was grateful to be rid of him. Sloane was hunched over in shock, without moving her head her eyes slowly looked up at the large man. He stared back at her with piercing blue eyes for just a moment before she summoned the courage to turn and reach for the door once more. Just as she grabbed the handle she felt a powerful hand grab the back of her head and force her face into the thick glass.

The Franklin Global success story fell to the ground with a thud having just experienced the very beginning of her punishment.

Chapter 11

The full moon provided more light than normal at the warehouse. Sarah smoked a cigarette on the front steps, waiting for her perpetually insufficient father figure to come home. Coming here was obviously unhealthy, she thought, but what else was she supposed to do? The rest of the world felt like a well rehearsed play, all put on for her and she wasn't interested in seeing the show.

It had been six years since she first returned to that place, nervously knocking on the doors after she had aged out of her last foster home at eighteen years old. It took several attempts before he finally answered the door long enough to tell her to go away. Sarah figured that if she was persistent enough then he might finally talk to her. What was it, she wondered, that she even wanted? She asked herself this question often but never really had an answer until recently.

This series of robberies invited a new sense of purpose into her world. Somehow she took an attack on a piece of her home very personally and she thought that maybe she could finally understand what exactly made her savior tick. The need for justice ran surprisingly hot through her veins but she knew there was nothing that she could do. It seemed insane or perhaps even immoral to have a direct connection to The Good Samaritan Killer and do nothing about it.

She had always been uncomfortable with that name, "The Good Samaritan." She was familiar with the verse that inspired the nickname but she knew the man and if whoever coined that moniker had ever met him they likely wouldn't be able to stomach associating him with the biblical representation of selfless kindness. He was that, she thought, but something about the name made him seem weak and she didn't support it. Had the man she knew been around back then he would have picked up the certain man from the street in Jerico but shortly after you can be sure he would have found and decapitated whoever put him there, and the priest and levite would have been right behind them.

Bright lights flashed across her face and Sarah jumped to her feet as a black sedan pulled into the gravel parking lot. The Good Samaritan frowned in judgment as he exited his vehicle and saw the young woman waiting for him.

"Go home," he said coldly as he rounded the car and popped the trunk.

"I need to ask you something," she said with desperation as the trunk flew open, revealing a woman bound and gagged with a sizable gash on her forehead. Sarah looked shocked for a moment but quickly moved on. Later she would reflect on that moment and wonder if she should have been more disturbed than she was but it was certainly something she had seen before.

"No," he said with his typical icy tone as he pulled Sloane out of the trunk and dropped her to the ground.

"There's a shop uptown. Gets knocked over by the same two guys every week, cops won't do anything. Neighbors say no one else will, they're too scared." Sarah tried to avoid making eye contact with Sloane who was silently begging for her help and astonished that this young woman didn't seem disturbed by what she was witnessing.

The Good Samaritan closed the trunk, hoisted Sloane over his shoulder and proceeded to the front doors as Sarah persisted. "After the shop started getting knocked over, the guy who helps run it, he lost all his business. He had a sick kid. Kid died a few months ago because they couldn't pay for the treatments."

After the doors swung open, Sloane's limp body was tossed to the floor as if The Good Samaritan were doing his chores and she was just a basket of laundry. With an exhausted sigh he turned to Sarah, "Where's the shop?"

Sarah's heart leapt with excitement, "MLK. Near fifth. Lucky Saver."

Without acknowledging her statement he stepped inside and slammed the door behind him. Sarah heard the woman's body slide away from the door, kicking as much as she was able to. Her heart still racing, Sarah looked in every direction as if looking for someone who could confirm for her what just happened. He listened, even if in his own way he really listened.

For Sarah, this felt like the start of something beautiful.

———

Night time downtown was always surprisingly quiet as most of the buildings were office buildings and there were very few condos or night time entertainment options. As a good number of the buildings contained government offices The Good Samaritan often chose the area for his body dumping.

Less pedestrian traffic meant less onlookers, but it also meant that the normally sleepy streets were now populated by a less appealing group of residents. The steps of city hall, normally peaceful after dark, were alive with lights and voices. When Jackson arrived, he pushed his way past the small crowd of news crew and homeless people.

Jackson flashed his badge to the officer holding back the crowd and slipped under the police line. The large concrete steps spread sixty feet across and climbed up at least 30 feet to the top, it was a grand entrance which he has always thought was a little too self-important for this level of government. The police tape stretched all the way across the bottom, leaving the steep incline completely bare with the exception of the gruesome scene he had come to see.

The young detective was used to murder at this point, it didn't take too long to get past some of the worse side effects of seeing a dead body. But The Good Samaritan had a certain signature for his victims and they were rarely easy to look upon. Sprawled out on the concrete steps was a priest, at least Jackson presumed the collar around his neck was truly his but it was hard to be sure because the man wasn't wearing anything else. Jesus, he thought, what did a priest do?

The dead body before him had been brutalized, there wasn't a single square inch without an injury. Jackson hated the thought of it but he had to give credit for the almost creative variety of injuries ranging from burns to stab wounds and incisions. Just looking at the horrid collage of violence was enough to know how much pain this person went through, as was the case with all of these victims.

Jackson looked around, wondering what Detective Corbin would do if he were here while also acknowledging how upset he would be once he learned that he missed it. He knelt down and took a few photos with his phone, stepping in all directions and excusing himself as he worked around the crime scene technicians. There was very little blood on the stairs despite all the wounds and a prominent bullet entry point in the middle of the victim's forehead. The smell was putrid, he had to step back into the fresh air.

The detective approached Ashton Murray, the medical examiner, who stood nearby taking notes and occasionally barking orders to the techs. "How long has he been cold?"

"Hard to say for sure," Murray said without looking up. "Three days, at least."

Jackson was puzzled, "Are you sure? Why wait three days?"

Murray didn't appreciate being questioned, especially when the stench made some things a little obvious. He looked up at Jackson, "Has there ever been a point in this case where you didn't have more questions than answers?"

Jackson frowned, "Yeah, it's definitely him."

The body had been tossed into its final resting place, the arm spread awkwardly to the sides and the head was looking up, almost as if he was hoping for some help from someone at the top of the stairs. Only about ten feet from the street, Jackson tried to imagine what it would take to physically get the corpse where it lay. If he remembered correctly, The Good Samaritan usually dumped his victims from a moving vehicle, which made the security cameras on these buildings relatively useless. Corbin had never been able to make an ID through the windows and the plate was always removed.

Near the bottom step there was a black mark that streaked a few inches across the edge. Jackson inspected it carefully, then glanced just past the police line. There were more marks beneath the feet of the bums and the reporters who were badgering him with questions as he tried to work.

"Hey!" Jackson shouted to the closest officer. "Get these people back and find something to block this area off."

"Sir?" the officer was confused, noting where the body clearly was.

"Look, dipshit." Jackson pointed to the sidewalk and a few members of the crowd stepped back to see what he was talking about. "Whatever numb nuts taped this off did it too close. The killer drove up on the sidewalk, see? OK go on, get! Everybody, back!"

The crowd slowly shuffled backwards at his command, revealing a set of tire tracks on the sidewalk. A few officers scrambled to rearrange the barrier. Jackson took another photo of the tracks and stood behind them, imagining the moment that the vehicle jumped the curb and swung the door open. He wondered if the car even slowed down as the victim crashed to the steps and sped off.

In this town you never knew whether a murder scene was going to be a "Good Samaritan" Case. The initial investigations were randomly assigned and these were always the hardest.

Chapter 12

Tap Seventeen was not the best restaurant downtown but it was considered to be close and had won the "Best Tapas" three years in a row. The owners had hoped for the best steak but were happy to take the publicity and decided to shift their marketing towards the tapas to capitalize on it. The location, decor and menu kept the dining room filled with people from the many neighboring fortune 500 level companies and the tips were fantastic.

Sarah leaned against the wall of the back door by the alley smoking a cigarette. It was quiet in the alley, an unusual sort of peace that hid amongst the trash and feral cats. Working in a restaurant was fine, that wasn't the problem, it was constantly being surrounded by people that got under her skin. People talk too much.

She had applied for the job reluctantly more than two years ago and at this point had no intention of moving on. While she hated the idea of doing something so social every single day, she had to come to terms with the fact that she really did need money to survive and she didn't have any skills that qualified her for most other jobs. Plus, she had to admit, she was good at it. That wasn't something she had ever been able to explain really but she was fully capable of taking orders without a pad, keeping track of what was in progress in the kitchen and doing all of that without feeling pressured.

Likely the best part of the job was listening. Sarah caught two to three sentence fragments of hundreds of conversations every day. Most dining room chatter was boring but the disgusting upper class scum that came into

Tap Seventeen always took the opportunity to trash talk whoever didn't make it to lunch that day. In a way Sarah got to know each of them quite well over time in a very one sided relationship and had been ranking them on which was the worst human being.

"Sarah!" a gruff voice shouted from inside, "Order up!"

She rolled her eyes and tossed her cigarette before heading back in. "Fuck you, Chet. You just plated the greens, the strip has another forty seconds on it and Alice is only just now coming out with the ceviche and you fuckin' know it."

Sarah approached Chet to wait for the dishes to be slid on to the counter before her, he didn't respond out of frustration that her timing seemed to be exactly correct. The kitchen was an overwhelming environment to say the least, an overheated symphony of stream and stress. Sarah preferred the quiet of the alley as often as she could throughout the day.

Chet slid the plates onto the counter, "You don't know everything, girl."

She smiled at him sarcastically and turned to deliver her order. Pushing through the swinging doors she entered the world of affluence where you could cut the white privilege with a knife. The decor was Italian inspired despite very few Italian dishes, the chairs were all exceptionally comfortable and the bar was fully stocked with top shelf liquors. Even the house whisky was twenty five dollars a glass.

Sarah approached table number six and dropped the plates with a forced smile. These two weren't the worst, only numbers twenty eight and thirty two on the list of terrible humans.

"......up twenty three percent in the last two years, it's fucking amazing." said Thirty Two.

"Good thing they fired that bitch. Could you imagine if she still had her claws in this?" Twenty Eight was quick to respond.

Sarah waited for a breath to insert herself, "Please enjoy."

Asshole number twenty eight waved her off without making eye contact and the two continued their gossiping. Sarah had always wondered if it'd be possible to get some of these people in the same room as a flock of ladies fresh from the hair salon and see who could talk more shit. She stepped away from their table and caught the eye of number eleven on the list who raised his empty beer glass. Sarah nodded and changed course to the bar.

Casey Baron was finishing up a round of Kamikazes as she approached. "Jai Alai for table four," she said, wanting to keep things brief.

The young bartender smiled, happy for the opportunity to talk with the one person who didn't want to talk to anybody. "What are you doing tonight?"

"Got a date," Sarah said quickly and dismissively.

Casey played along and acted intrigued as another server took the shots away. "Oh yeah?"

"Oh yeah, big date."

He got out a fresh beer glass and approached her, she noted that this was in the opposite direction of the tap where he was supposed to be. "With who?" he pushed.

"You wouldn't know him." she said after considering for a moment. "He's a cop. Also one of those influencer guys that teach other guys how to pleasure women. Very sexy. I'm pretty excited about it."

"Uh huh," Casey decided that was enough of the show and he turned to fill the glass with the draught that he always found too hoppy for his tastes. "You know, one day you're going to decide that being alone all the time and being a bitch to anyone who's nice to you is not as good as actually being with someone who likes you."

He placed the full glass on the bar in front of her.

"You gonna save me, Casey?" she teased.

"Alright, alright," he turned and moved on to his next drink order.

"Oh, but I need your help! I have so much angst." She picked up the beer and turned away.

"Bye, Sarah." Casey said, shaking his head.

"The angst! It cripples me so!" Sarah continued her performance as she left the bar and re-entered the dining room. Four more hours of this before she went home and rested comfortably in her world of curated pleasures.

––––––––––

John Corbin walked through the doors of Saint Mary's Hospital where he had not been since his daughter was born. While the facility itself was well updated with all the modern conveniences, it was an old building and the front facade had been preserved which created a sort of time travel feeling as you stepped into a world of blue tile floors and glass walls.

Just as he stepped inside he heard the sound of local news playing on a nearby television in the lobby, *"... and another body has been found carrying the infamous signature of the man who has been dubbed "The Good Samaritan". This, of course, being the person or persons responsible for the series of murders that seem to be aimed specifically at the criminal community."*

"Son of a bitch," Corbin said out loud, irritated that he was learning of a new murder through the local news.

The television continued, *"The most recent victim has been identified as Carmine Ellis, a Priest of a local Roman Catholic church. As usual, a package of evidence was left with the body, incriminating the man of his crimes. The police have not yet released what those crimes are."*

Corbin shook his head and walked up to the front desk.

"Here to see Rachel Corbin, please," he said without smiling as he approached the visitors check-in. Corbin handed the employee his ID and the pocket-sized printer minted a visitor's sticker with his name on it. Corbin was directed to the oncology building and handed a paper map to assist him.

It was a large campus and the walk to room five-six-one would be a long one, giving Corbin plenty of time to think. Rachel was an incredible mother, that had been true from before they even had kids. Her instinct for nurture had been clear even with the neighborhood kids when they first got married fourteen years before. She was always a planner and it wasn't long after they first got together that she had their first twenty years mapped out including the two children within three years of marriage. Everything did turn out exactly as she planned.

What wasn't in the plan, Corbin reminded himself, was the young cop who would put work before anything else. She had worked it all out and he was so enamored with her beauty and intelligence that he said yes to just about anything she ever asked, not taking a moment to recognize that little of what she had in mind would play nicely with his career path.

What did fit well was the church. Rachel had been raised a devout Christian and started inviting him to services shortly after they started dating. Corbin hadn't been since his grandmother died when he was seven, she had always been the religious leader of the family and without her the practice slipped away. He and his parents would go back now and then but largely on the "important" days like Easter and Christmas.

When Rachel brought him to her church it wasn't like bringing up the past and getting back into a habit, which was what he expected. The services Corbin attended as a child felt like a chore and never meant much but the people at Rachel's church welcomed him gladly. He felt warm and safe there and his relationship with God grew stronger.

When Rachel let him know that he had missed his last chance to put their family first and left, he assumed his faith would slip once again. To Corbin's surprise it brought him closer to God and he felt comforted by the one constant still left in his life. Not able to see Rachel each Sunday, he found a new church and kept his relationship with God alive and well. In a world where so much loss surrounded him every day and now the divorce, it was fair to say that having kept his faith was what kept Corbin breathing.

And now here he was, walking down the hallways of the oncology building at Saint Mary's hospital on a Tuesday evening. Rachel's plan had been a good one and they did have two daughters who were now almost entirely without a father. As the distance between Corbin and room five six one got smaller, his pace slowed. The phone call he had gotten this morning made his heart freeze and he could barely stand to take the next few steps.

He stepped just inside the open door and cautiously peered inside. Rachel was lying in the hospital bed. She had no hair, had lost what looked like ten pounds and her normally soft brown skin was pale and looked cold. Asleep in the chair beside her was Vanessa, Rachel's sister, who had not so much as looked Corbin in the eye since the divorce.

Rachel noticed him as he walked in the door and smiled just enough to make him feel like he had permission to enter. "Hi," he said with some exhaustion.

"Hi," she responded. Their conversations used to be so much more vibrant.

"What, um...what's the latest?" he asked, genuinely not knowing what any of their futures looked like. He knew it was stage four breast cancer but it apparently was spreading so quickly that checking in every two weeks wasn't enough for him to have any idea how bad things were.

"The latest? Well, the Jaguars lost again, John. I mean who's surprised?" she chuckled lightly.

It was incredible, Corbin thought, that she had the ability to make jokes at a time like this. More surprisingly, possibly, was that this highly intelligent woman who had the poor misfortune of being born in Jacksonville, Florida still held on to her status as a diehard fan. He smiled and took a step closer.

She knew he was going to insist on a real answer so she volunteered one, "We decided to stop the treatments. I feel like crap, I look like crap. There was a chance but that's been used up so we're aiming for comfort now I guess."

At that moment, Vanessa opened her eyes and noticed Corbin in the room. Rachel smiled at her and nodded as her sister took the cue to leave. "I'll go check on the kids," she said as she collected her purse and left, still managing to not look at Corbin once.

"It's not going to be long at this point," said Rachel, still showing that cool confidence but with tears in her eyes.

Even though everything had fallen apart and he only had himself to blame, Corbin had never stopped loving her. Suddenly he couldn't look at her anymore and he moved to the end of her bed, leaning on the footboard for support. He could hear his own heartbeat in his chest and felt his pulse pounding in his neck.

"Where are the kids?" he managed to get out.

"Down the hall. They have a nursery kind of thing. Jean is too old for it and hates it there but we didn't have a choice this morning," she said with a bit of her humor back in her voice.

Corbin's mind raced, planning ahead the next one, five, twenty years. This can't be true, he thought, she is what is best for them. He knew that their best chance at life was to be raised by their mother and no one else, certainly not him.

"What is not going to be long at this point?" he asked, still not able to look at her.

She didn't answer right away. Rachel knew that he still loved her and if she was honest with herself she would admit that she felt the same. "It will be over soon. And I'll be in a better place. It's part of His plan. I just have to trust it."

Corbin was noticeably distressed by her last statement. "Sorry, I know you hate that," she offered.

It was true, as much as Corbin had found a home in the church he had always hated the "plan" that so many people referred to. He always felt it was perfectly easy to love God, praise Jesus, love one another and do everything you're taught to do without feeling the need to blame everything that was too hard to handle on the "plan." He had always told Rachel that they all had the choice to live their own life and take it any direction, that there was no master plan to pre-determine it all. If there were then it would mean that it wasn't his fault he let his family fall apart, it would mean that Rachel dying was somehow good for anybody and it would mean that the psychopath murdering people in some warehouse was doing it because he was "supposed to."

"Yeah," he said in reply, standing himself up straight again.

"Can you take them for a while?" she asked.

He looked surprised but not because he didn't expect it. It was the confidence in her voice. This must have been her last resort but for her to ask at all knowing better than anyone that he was not qualified to be a full time parent was truly shocking.

"Y-yeah. Of course. I've got 'em." he replied, trying to assure her that he was up to the task. "Um, where is the uh..."

"Down the hall that way. On the left." She did her best to smile.

Corbin turned to leave the room and stopped himself at the doorway. He didn't turn back to her, not knowing what to say, he only knew that something must be said before he left. He wondered if this was the last time he would see her. The love of his life, both his best friend and greatest failure. He had disappointed her so many times, was this his last chance to do right by her?

"John," said Rachel, sparing him from his responsibility to speak first.

Corbin turned to her and looked into her beautiful eyes.. Rachel had kind eyes, those hadn't changed at all, but they were filled with tears now. No longer able to hold it back, she wept for a brief moment before saying what she had to say. "Tell them...tell them I love them, ok?"

Corbin nodded like he understood but she cut him off before he could speak, "Every day. I tell them every day and every night. I can't tell them anymore so you do it. You pray with them and tell them I love them. Because I ca-"

She held her hand out to him, not asking for him to take it but to steady herself. "Because I can't. And it's your job now."

There was no right thing to say. "I will," is what he managed to get out.

"John," she begged him with her eyes.

"Every day. You love them," he reassured her. She nodded and rested her head.

Corbin left the room and proceeded down the hallway, wiping tears from his cheeks. If that wasn't the hardest part, the next step would be. He loved his girls and he was nearly certain that they knew that. But every other weekend wasn't much, especially when nearly half the time something came up and he had to cancel. The girls certainly weren't strangers to him but sometimes it felt that way.

As he approached the daycare room, he first saw Vanessa through the window who immediately noted his presence. He had always felt he deserved a certain degree of disdain or even punishment for the choices he had made but sometimes thought Vanessa's coldness was a bit disproportionate. There were worse dads than him.

Once he passed through the doorway he finally saw his two little girls. Jean was thirteen years old now and understood the world plenty well, Bella was only nine and clung to an optimistic perspective of her life that felt younger than her age. Jean usually did her best to seem as independent as possible but today her hair was pulled up into a bun just like Bella's. The younger of the two noticed Corbin just as he entered the room.

"Daddy!" She ran to him and wrapped her arms around him.

Jean waited for her sister to appreciate her moment, then stood and hugged her father.

"You okay?" she asked.

That was Jean, Corbin thought. She was too mature before she was eight, add in a divorce, an absent father and a tragic cancer diagnosis and she was practically old enough to rent a car. Corbin enjoyed the embrace of his two daughters at the same time, then knelt down to them.

"Yeah, I'm okay sweetheart. How 'bout you guys? Have you been here long?" he asked.

Bella, the perpetual optimist, responded first. "I got to get up super early this morning and see everything while the lights were all off. Even Starbucks was closed, Daddy."

Corbin smiled. He was sure there was a lot to talk about and was even more sure that he wasn't qualified to facilitate the conversation. But this wasn't the time. He took another moment to enjoy Bella's smile and Jean's calm confidence before ushering them out of the room. He nodded to Vanessa as he left and she spoke to him for the first time in years.

"John," she said sharply.

He turned and made sure the girls were out of the room. There was no doubt that Jean would make sure she was still close enough to hear.

"You realize what is at stake here, don't you?" the interrogation began. "She's gonna die. That's all there is. And that leaves these girls with you."

"Yeah, I get that, Vanessa," he responded, trying to find the balance between being offended and agreeing with her skepticism.

"I thought she'd pick me. I asked her to. She didn't. So they have you. Is she making a mistake?"

Corbin considered the question for a brief moment. "You know, I don't know what to tell you that would make you feel better because I'm wondering the same thing. But I'll tell you this:"

She glared into his eyes with pure distrust.

"Rachel is the smartest, kindest person I know. Yeah, she's right about this. She's always right."

Corbin left the room, not caring about what Vanessa had to say in response. When he stepped out into the hallway, he collected his girls and proceeded towards the elevators. Jean was now nearly up to his shoulders in height. As the elevator bell rang, Corbin had a thought that would ring in his mind for years to come. This was the day that everything changed.

———

From within the warehouse main floor, there was no daylight to be seen even though the extreme heat made it clear that the sun had been high in the sky for hours. Sloane Kelli sat in the wooden chair, coated several times over with a deep, dark red stain. Her hands and forearms were bound behind her with a rope that was old and tattered but still quite strong. A redness on her skin radiated for several inches from the rope.

The Good Samaritan entered the light, the shadows only revealing his emotionless face just inches at a time. He took a moment to observe the woman before him. She had been stripped of her clothes just as the priest had been, as they had all been. Her nude body was toned but filthy. He had only recently begun his work but already she had twelve puncture wounds in various places on her body and thirty percent of her skin was now bruised. He admired his work, considering this stage to be the base layer for what would eventually be an intricate tapestry of punishment.

"I'm sorry," begged Sloane, "I'm so sorry." Tears were now streaming from her eyes, wasting what little hydration she had left in her body.

Her tormentor was intrigued by this statement. The two had spent days together and so far she had only ever denied her involvement in the murder of Jeffery Weinstien. This was progress.

"I am so sorry," her begs for mercy had crumbled into sobs.

The man lowered his towering height to her level, kneeling before her. Unwilling to touch her, he picked up a pair of pliers from the floor and lifted her chin. "For what do you apologize?"

They locked eyes. Sloane met the gaze of the man that would certainly be her demise. "I killed that man." The words squeezed out of her mouth.

The Good Samaritan studied her face for a moment before responding, "Who?"

Sloane's heart stopped. This was the first moment she had noticed that she had no idea exactly who the man was. She had stolen a life and to this day had no idea who it was, not even a vague understanding of who he left behind or what his life had been. She had seen the news reports and they almost certainly must have identified him but she was so preoccupied with her own fears of being caught that she never heard it.

"Oh, Jesus. I don't know. I have no idea," she shared, hating herself.

Her host stood and proceeded to grab a tool from the table to her right. The tool was unusual looking, a sort of modified cat o' nine tails. A wooden handle was connected to nine short lengths of rope which would normally split off into three strands. This tool, however, had been customized with a single razor blade on the end of each rope. The Good Samaritan proceeded to circle his student and stopped behind her.

He carefully and slowly clarified to Sloane "His name was Walter. He was twenty eight. He was married. He was expecting a child."

For a moment Sloane took this information as a relief. She looked up, thankful that she could begin to make her own peace with what she had done. Suddenly, her extremities went cold as she felt a pain unlike any she had ever experienced. Behind her, on her pale shoulder blades, The Good Samaritan had whipped her with the cat o' nine tails. Four of the nine razor blades had embedded themselves within her skin. He proceeded to pull the rope across her skin from right to left, the blades digging deeper as he did so. When he reached her left shoulder blade he ripped the blades from her skin, sending a few slices of muscle tissue to the floor. Sloane screamed in pain, or at least she thought she did. In reality, she had forgotten how to emit any sound at all as the sensation shocked every nerve ending in her body.

He stepped around to her front again, grabbing a large iron fireplace poker from the table as he did. Without hesitation, he thrusted the poker into the meat between Sloane's neck and shoulder. For this, she did allow a weak scream to emit. The poker pushed through her flesh and was done so with such force that it pierced the chair and burst through the back support.

The Good Samaritan knelt once more and found her eyes. "What....was his name?"

Amidst all the pain, Sloane could not find the strength to speak. "Wa....W," was all she could force out which only frustrated The Good Samaritan who further plunged the poker deeper until the handle pressed against her shoulder.

Just then, his phone rang and he stepped away to answer it, leaving Sloane in the shock of realizing that this man owned a cell phone just like anyone else.

"Yes?" The Good Samaritan answered. Sloane could hear a man's voice on the other line and studied her captor as he listened. After a brief and one-sided conversation he hung up the phone and turned back to her. He seemed almost frustrated as his schedule had apparently been interrupted. With spectacular force, the beast of a man kicked her in the chest. Sloane immediately coughed up a mouthful of blood as her chair slid backwards into the darkness.

Chapter 13

John Corbin pushed his way past uniformed officers in the busy precinct hallway in search of Detective Jackson. He reflected on his coworker's youth and made a mental note to give him the benefit of the doubt before he chose to pull his weapon. With the limited amount of time he had left on this case, he couldn't stomach the fact that a fresh crime scene had made its way to the news before he even knew about it.

He had taken the girls to school this morning for the first time and it came with more challenges than he was prepared for. Thankful that the school system provides free babysitting five days a week, he still had to learn what the travel time between two schools was. Jean told him that he should sign them up for bus service in his neighborhood if they were going to be with him for a while and once again she proved to be mature beyond her years.

Corbin spotted Jackson at the far end of the squad room. "Jackson!" he shouted.

Jackson snapped around and looked relieved to see the senior detective. "Where the hell have you been?"

"It's complicated. What the fuck is going on?" Corbin was admittedly relieved to learn that at least Jackson had been trying to find him.

"What do you mean?"

"I mean why the hell am I hearing on the damn local news that there's another victim? I'm the lead investigator on this case and the crime scene was cleaned out before I even got there, yeah?"

Jackson wasn't thrilled with the accusation, "Well that's what happens when a body gets dumped in front of city hall. John, you said not to bother you, you said you were going to see your kids or whatever. They okay?"

"Yeah, I mean no. They're fine, yeah but things aren't ok." Corbin blurted out but this wasn't the topic he wanted to discuss. "But yeah, I meant don't bother me for small shit, not something like this!"

"Okay, I'm sorry. But look, you didn't miss anything, I got everything you need." Jackson reached for his phone. "You're such an asshole, you make me drag my ass out of bed for every one of these things, I know how you do it by now. I got everything you need, just the way you like it. Photos and everything."

Corbin calmed himself, taking a moment to be mildly impressed.

"Except for the brooding," Jackson continued, "I didn't do any brooding or like randomly accusing coworkers of shit. Should I have done that?"

The young detective searched for a smile without success and then proceeded to show the crime scene report to Corbin. It didn't exactly showcase the same efficiency that Corbin preferred but he had to admit that the report was well rounded. Jackson had even found what almost passed as a rare mistake by the killer.

The tracks that had been found on the sidewalk were unusual. They weren't unique as far as their make or model so they'd never be able to track down the vehicle that way but the fact that he would be so reckless as to jump the curb was unlike him. Even if they could find details on the vehicle, he had proven over the years to have access to a variety of highly ignorable cars. Every once in a while one could recognize a car in the security footage but sending out an APB for a black Honda Civic was a tall order.

Jackson and Corbin spent the day combing through the evidence and studying the photos for any missed details. For Jackson it was refreshing to be treated almost as if he were an equal, as much as he didn't want to admit it. About thirty minutes after three, Corbin looked at his watch and rushed out the door. Bella was picked up from school forty minutes late.

Smithworks, LLC made its home in a large building on the northern outskirts of the city. Twenty years ago, when its owner started the business, the area had been almost entirely farmland. In recent years the city had stretched its legs and now engulfed the impressive factory on all sides including a grocery store, several condo buildings and at least three options for frozen yogurt.

The building itself was easy to miss, featuring no distinctive features at all. On the rare occasion that a vendor or technician had to visit the business in person, they almost always had to call and ask where it was, only to be surprised that they somehow missed such a large structure. There were several joggers in the area that knew the building well and a few regular customers at the neighboring kava shop that would sometimes wonder what happened behind those large, gray doors.

The Good Samaritan entered through the rear entrance, always making a point to keep his presence as subtle as possible. As he passed through the main factory floor along the back wall several employees turned and took notice of their employer. His appearances were so rare and brief that spotting him was always something of a shock, almost as if they were spotting Willy Wonka making his way through the Inventing Room.

The massive rows of machines stretched down the length of the factory floor, each one surrounded by a team of technicians reminiscent of works found in old depression era photographs. If an onlooker outside were to catch a glimpse of the interior they would be filled with burning questions about products that were manufactured there. The truth was far less mysterious than any of them would hope.

From the beginning Smithworks manufactured basic plastic items, essentials for the home. There was a time, in fact, that The Good Samaritan thought he may be living a normal life. When his father passed just a few years prior he was left with a modest inheritance. Combined with his life savings, he invested in the business with every intention of choosing a simple day to day routine until he died. There was never any dream of joining the plastics industry, no Mr. Maguire to mentor him, it was simply the logical choice in a market that had a demand. There was no limit to the demand for plastics from the smallest component to an automobile to the structural support of the latest children's toy.

In the last two decades as the market had evolved, molding technology had advanced and in the meteoric rise of Amazon, Smithworks became a highly profitable entity with minimal supervision. The Good Samaritan had hired a CEO named Jerry Eichenbaum once his responsibilities to police the criminals that the system had given a free pass began taking up too much of his time. Jerry was a hard worker, honest and kind to the employees. His salary was high enough that he never asked questions about The Good

Samaritan's daily schedule and only ever contacted him in cases of emergency.

Today was one of those emergencies. An order had been returned due to a defect which was not entirely unusual except this one was worth well into the six figures and the responsible party had not yet revealed themselves. Jerry knew his employer and was certain that he would want the person or person to be held accountable so he called right away.

Jerry had occupied the largest office, ever since he was hired fifteen years ago, surprised that the owner was satisfied with the small office next door. He would eventually learn that the small office was rarely occupied anyway. Jerry was always intimidated as the large man entered his office, just barely clearing the doorway as he approached Jerry.

"Hello, sir. I appreciate you coming on such short notice," Jerry said as he hurried around his desk with his hand extended.

"Of course," replied The Good Samaritan as he shook Jerry's hand. "Which machine?"

"Yes, sir. We're headed for the floor, section twelve. Right this way."

Jerry ushered him down to the factory floor where the suspects would be called into a private room and judgment would be made. The workers of section twelve were mostly young, totalling seven men and two women. The machine they were operating that month was manufacturing several components that fit into the computer system of the latest electric vehicle. Most orders in the factory were between eight and fifteen thousand units, this order totalled well over thirty thousand units.

It would eventually be determined that a small error in the chemical mixture of the plastic itself caused a hairline fracture to occur in almost every unit. This led to a complete failure in the operating systems of the vehicle and the entire line had to be recalled. The financial magnitude of the mistake was catastrophic and Jerry knew it. Only a few times during his tenure at Smithworks did a mistake of this magnitude take place.

The CEO watched through the glass of the conference room window as the owner of the company invited the entire team to have a seat around the table. As far as Jerry could tell, not a single word was spoken. The Good Samaritan looked each one of them in the eyes, some of whom were unwilling to meet his gaze.

Finally, their employer spoke and one of the men rested his head on the table in tears. The other employees were excused from the room and one by one they marched out of the room and returned to their positions on the line. Jerry stepped into the room to see the young man sobbing at his uncertain future.

The Good Samaritan stood and approached Jerry, "See to it that he is given a severance package. Fifteen percent his salary."

"'Severance package?'" Jerry couldn't believe there would be any mercy for this man. The Good Samaritan turned to meet Jerry's eyes. Without a word spoken, Jerry knew it was a mistake to question his employer and he quickly nodded.

The mysterious business owner left immediately following the young line worker's departure and the day continued like any other work day. During their lunch hour, the workers would discuss their varying theories about how he typically spent his days ranging from agoraphobic recluse to some sort of vampire that occasionally was able to walk in the daylight. Jerry sat at his desk, still a little shaken from the look he had received from his employer earlier and expressed a sigh of thankfulness that these visits were so infrequent.

Chapter 14

At the twenty third precinct, Jean and Bella read a comic book together on the floor at the end of Corbin's desk. The busy squad room was aware of their presence, occasionally offering a smile in their direction. It was refreshing to see young, innocent faces in a place where so much darkness passed through. Corbin glanced down at them as he prepared to make his next phone call. Jean had always been a fan of comic books even back when all her friends told her they were just for boys. She was partial to the anti-hero storylines like Wolverine and Deadpool but had a special place in her heart for strong female characters. Bella was just beginning to appreciate the complexities of the stories, but had always enjoyed the artistry of the illustrations.

Corbin opened an old case file and found the contact information for Linda Heartstrong. Her husband had been reported missing nine years ago and the search went on for three weeks until he suddenly appeared on the sidewalk of the sixteenth precinct missing most of his fingers and a pulse. She had refused to speak with previous detectives, so he knew how this conversation would go but in fairness he had never reached out to her before. As he began dialing he rehearsed his very best "nice guy" voice in his head.

A woman answered and Corbin smiled despite not being seen, "Yes, Hi. Is this Linda Heartstrong?" A quiet confirmation came from the voice on the phone. "This is Detective John Corbin with the twenty third precinct. I am investigating the series of murders that we believe were related to Gary's death. Yes, well, we've recently come into some new evidence and I was wondering if you'd like to meet me tomorrow and answer a few questions. Well, how about Wednesday?"

Jean glanced up at her father, hearing the struggle in his voice. She had a hard time processing her feelings about him at times but seeing him in this element was refreshing. He really did care about these people. It was good to know that he cared about someone, even if it wasn't her and Bella.

"Any time next week?" her father continued. "Do you have time now? I see. Ok, you too."

Corbin hung up the phone in disappointment. It was truly remarkable how many witnesses and victims were living and breathing out there in the city and how they were all unwilling to come forward. The psychological hold this man had on them was nothing short of paranormal.

Suddenly the dominating presence of Captain Morton could be felt and Corbin looked up to see the large man with his hands in his pockets, looking straight ahead. Without making eye contact the Captain said, "See you in my office?"

"Shit," Corbin whispered to himself as his superior walked off without a response. He stood and tapped the shoulder of a female officer. "Do you mind?" he asked as he gestured to the children,

She smiled and nodded as he began the long walk to the other side of the room. Corbin had always been fascinated that parents in general were so completely comfortable allowing women to keep an eye on their kids. He had had front row seats to some of the worst crimes involving children and it was true that absolutely the majority were committed by men. There is a violent nature that comes along with the male psyche and sometimes it seems that the only good men are the ones who can resist it. But women were responsible for over thirty percent of kidnappings so it wasn't exactly a sure thing when you left your children in their care. But, he supposed, you have to go with the odds.

Corbin slowly closed the Captain's door behind him as he entered. Morton stood behind his desk with his hands still in his pockets, he maintained a calm demeanor that Corbin was certain was masking a considerable amount of rage. Morton had always embraced the cheesy eighties stereotype of an action movie police captain, it was entirely too often that Corbin felt a kinship with Martin Riggs as he sat in this office.

"You must be out of your Goddamn mind," Morton said while stubbornly holding onto his smile. "This ain't a fuckin' daycare center, detective! Jesus Christ, did someone seriously have to say that to you?" The smile was gone.

"My ex-wife is sick," Corbin pleaded. "She can't take care of them, and I'm still working on the aftercare thing with the school. But I'll get it worked out. Please, come on, it's just for a few days."

The silence in the room was deafening as Morton geared up for his response. "You've worked under me for three years, let me ask you something. Have I ever sent you a Christmas card? Wished you a happy birthday? Told you to have a happy fucking new year? No. So, if you're asking me whether I'm going to be a nice guy today and let you treat my squad room like a fuckin' Chuck E Cheese, then my answer to you should be pretty fuckin' clear! It is well outside of the guidelines of conduct for this office and I won't have a senior detective showing everybody how to break the rules!"

He wasn't wrong. It wasn't a question of whether it was unprofessional or whether a building filled with criminals was the place for children. Corbin had hoped he could play the single dad card which seemed to work with just about everybody but Morton. He nodded in acknowledgment that his superior was right.

"Captain, can I get an extension on the case? The kids..." Corbin immediately regretted the words as soon as that exited his mouth.

Surprisingly, Morton allowed time for a few breaths before the vein in his temple burst in response to the bold request. "Look ... John. You gotta forget about this case, I don't care how close you are."

The new, almost soothing tone sounded like a trap. "In a perfect world, we'd catch this guy, but there are people above me making decisions here, okay? If you don't wrap it up, I have to transfer you. And I don't want to do that because you're one of my best cops. But something ain't right in your head lately, and I'm not the only one seein' it. I told you your time is running out. I'm standing by it. Don't fuck this up."

Corbin looked up at the former linebacker, not sure how to react after such a change in leadership styles. The Captain gestured to the door, "Now, go on."

The detective stood and left the room with the weight of an unsolvable case, two children who needed him and a captain possibly struggling with borderline personality disorder resting on his tired shoulders.

The warm coffee mug felt comforting in her hands. Cheryl O'Connell had left hot coffee behind years ago and preferred her caffeine to come iced now.

Her mug was filled with soup that day, it had become the only food that she could keep down plus it had the added bonus of being a classic comfort food. Comfort had been in short supply lately.

Since the death of her husband, Cheryl had not slept for more than an hour or so and eating had become a serious chore. Friends and family had been kind enough to supply her with a seemingly never ending stream of food and she didn't have the heart to tell them to stop because it was all just wasting away. Normally a beautiful woman, her face looked like it had aged fifteen years in the last few weeks. She had finally accepted Walter's passing had actually happened but felt it would be years before making peace with it.

Cheryl reminded herself that she had had a responsibility during that time which she failed to accomplish. She had been trusted as the safe space for Walter's child to grow and when she stopped sleeping and eating nature punished her for her negligence. She had lost the baby earlier that week, the pain of which had been severely numbed. As much as she struggled with the reality of Walter's death, she knew it would be years before she could handle the loss of their child.

She peered through the lace curtains of her front windows, studying the vultures parked out front. Cheryl had spent most of her life with quiet opinions about the local news media, never willing to watch as the terrible news from places so close seemed to evaporate the joy out of a room. Now that she was the subject of their post commercial break story, her distaste for them had grown to hatred.

Ever since Walter's body had been found at the bottom of a ditch, murdered by what was most likely a drunk driver, the vans had been showing up nearly every day. They lived in a suburb and tragedy out there was less common than the big city and twice as entertaining. Just imagine how much they would drool if they learned about the miscarriage. Cheryl had never issued a statement or even been willing to speak to them which seemed to only make matters worse, almost as if the jackals were hungry and must be fed if she wanted them to leave.

No, she told herself. She would never allow Walter's memory to become a top story. She took another sip of soup and walked into her kitchen. Their home was not large but it had everything they needed, complete with a small hot tub in the back that Walter had been planning to fix for about three years. The O'Connell home had always been well lit at night, but Cheryl had lost the energy that flipping each switch required and she now preferred the dark. Besides, with the lights off she could still keep an eye on the activity in her front yard without being seen.

The electric buzz of her cell phone vibrating on the dark wood dining table shot through the house. She walked into the room as the small screen illuminated the dark space. There was a text message waiting for her, without picking it up she read the message.

[You don't know me, but I am a friend.]

She suspected it was just another news desk.

[Your husband's killer is in my possession.]

Cheryl's grip on her warm mug tightened. Nothing could have prepared her for that.

[We have much to discuss, if you'd please call this number.]

She continued to stare at the phone. There was no way this was serious and if it was what kind of a psychopath would admit to kidnapping this way? A moment passed that felt like hours.

[Please.]

Something about the last message shook her. Did this person know that she was hesitating? She looked around the room frantically then rushed to each door and checked the locks. From the front door, she heard the phone vibrate once more. This time she held it in her hand.

[It's ok, Cheryl. I won't hurt you. I'm here for you. For Walter.]

Her world had been destroyed, her life stopped entirely. There had been a plan, it wasn't incredibly unique or surprising or special but it was a plan; have a child, grow old. And now the plan hadn't just been changed, it was gone. There was nothing of her old world left and Cheryl couldn't even begin to imagine how she would convince herself that life had purpose anymore.

Knowing that there was nothing left to lose, she lifted her phone and tapped the stranger's number. There was barely even a full ring before the other end picked up.

"Hello, Cheryl."

Chapter 15

Detective John Corbin pulled to a stop in front of a duplex in a part of town called Lake Clarke Estates. It wasn't the best neighborhood but there had been a time when he had planned to move the family there, the schools nearby were excellent according to Rachel. He took a look around as he exited the car and closed the door, wondering to himself if this would have been his street, if the girls would have played in the field across the way.

He stepped into the driveway, leaving behind his blue Honda Civic. Corbin was glad that he wasn't required to drive a squad car anymore but he often admitted to himself that the Civic did not exactly make the best first impression. The home he was visiting was a victim but when questioning a suspect, something with a little more intimidation power would have been nice. For this visit, however, his fuel efficient option would be just fine.

Maureen Stone had submitted her testimony five years ago after her son's killer was murdered. The statement had been brief but effective, very simply put she didn't know anything. Corbin knew that five years was a long time and sometimes things change. Witnesses can remember small things they left out years before and people who have been intimidated can find themselves with a renewed sense of safety if you use the right words. He had spent the week on the phone as he juggled Jean and Bella's schedule but now that the good people of the public school system were taking care of things for the next few hours there was a chance to make an in-person visit which was always better. He even managed to attend to some of his other cases that morning, all of which felt like rookie work compared to his usual routine.

He had spent so much time on this case that other murder cases were not just boring, he found himself unconsciously judgmental of that particular class of criminal. While the psychopath that had consumed his time for the last three years was no hero at least he had a purpose. So many murders were the result of stupidity, drunkenness or just pure hate. As he went through his paperwork that morning he found himself wishing that he was investigating a murderer with integrity. It was a disturbing thought, respecting the man, but he couldn't shake the thought.

Corbin knocked on the door and studied the molding around the door and windows as he waited. This could have been his front porch, he thought to himself, a considerable improvement.

"Who is it?" a woman's voice shouted through the door.

The voice already sounded irritated so Corbin put on his best nice guy smile in case there was a doorbell camera being watched, "Uh … Detective John Corbin. I'd like to ask you a few questions if you don't mind."

"About what?" the voice wasn't getting friendlier.

Corbin hesitated before offering a response. This was often where he would lose people and he sometimes wondered if it was better to lie and establish a connection first before being honest. He quietly said, "Your son."

There was a silence and once again the detective told himself that honesty can sometimes slow down an investigation. He was preparing to offer a more convincing response when the sound of deadbolts shot from the other side of the door. Maureen Stone revealed herself as the door opened. She was a bigger woman dressed in scrubs and looked as though she was about to leave for work.

"Badge," she said with just slightly more warmth in her voice than before the door had opened. Corbin quickly revealed his identification and she invited him inside her home.

———————

Detective Corbin and Maureen sat in a small room filled with plants and surrounded by windows on three sides. Sunlight filled the room and made it feel like a garden blessed by spring weather. Corbin had never seen anything like it inside a home and admired the care taken with each plant which were all in perfect health.

Maureen had started crying almost as soon as they began speaking. The sunlight pierced through her short dirty blonde hair as she quietly continued her story. "He was only seven. We were at the park. I looked away, I should have been paying attention. He took him. He took him so quickly, I had no idea. The police couldn't do anything, no evidence, no clues. And four days later..."

Tears took the words from her before she could speak them. She had told this story so many times before, first to the police then to friends and family and eventually to the many support groups she had joined. The words almost sounded rehearsed at this point and she had begun to worry that they seemed disingenuous after so long. Regardless of how it sounded, she had never been able to describe the state that her son's body had been found in.

"I would have paid any ransom," she continued. "I would have given anything. But that... monster didn't want anything but my little boy. He did... unspeakable things to him."

Maureen lost her ability to control her breathing through her tears and she began fighting past sharp breaths as she spoke. "Mutilated his little body. That man deserved everything that he got."

She stood and picked up a small water bottle, "Oh, I shouldn't have turned away."

Maureen began spraying mists of water onto the plants. Corbin admired the streams of light shining through the clouds of water before he spoke, "It wasn't your fau-"

"Don't!" Maureen snapped. Corbin was taken aback by the sudden scolding but he immediately understood. She calmed herself and continued, "Mr. Corbin, I've been told for years that it was not my fault. I'm not an idiot, I know I didn't kill my little boy but there was one person in charge of keeping him safe that day and it was me."

"Ma'am, I-"

"That's all I have to say." Maureen turned back to her quiet family of flora.

Corbin knew that there wasn't much more that he could say. This was yet another on a very long list of witnesses that either couldn't or wouldn't say anything. Once again, the incredible hold this man had on people made the investigation near impossible.

"Please, I just have a few more questions," he attempted.

"I'd really rather not, Detective. Because the body of my son's killer was found." The gentle spraying had stopped and she was now pruning stray leaves and dead limbs from the plants. As she spoke, her moves became faster and more aggressive, sending little green pieces falling to the ground. "He was laid out on the street beaten and shredded to bits with all the evidence you needed but couldn't find yourself. So that means you're not here to ask me about him. Either you're here to force me to relive my boy's death which seems incredibly cruel or you must be here to ask me whether or not I know exactly how that man died."

Corbin sat back in his chair, embarrassed to be called out so directly. It was incredible how often he felt like the bad guy during the course of investigating a serial killer.

"So, unless I'm the first person you talked to, I think you know my answer. My son deserved justice, and none of you could give it to him. Even if you had caught him first, that son of a bitch would be enjoying three square meals a day on my dollar right now. So I won't be helping you find the only person who cared enough to actually do something. You can let yourself out."

Maureen stormed out of the room, leaving Corbin alone in the suburban paradise. He stood and collected his folders that were never opened. As he walked through the front door and closed it he once again was reminded that had things been different he could have had a room filled with light to raise plants in. He didn't know how to do that but was confident that he could learn. Detective Corbin walked away from the duplex feeling defeated but with a renewed intention to take advantage of the one lead he had left.

———————

The address was in a part of town that Cheryl had never been to. As she drove where the stranger from her phone had directed her, she admitted to herself that it was likely one of the stupider things she had ever done. In a world where women couldn't feel safe walking to their car at night for fear of what hid in the shadows, it seemed incredibly naive to specifically seek out a man who openly admittedly to abducting another woman. But she felt she had no choice, this was about Walter and the police had gotten nowhere.

She parked her car in the gravel parking lot of a building that seemed to embody the very spirit of dark warnings. The street lights in every direction were dim but functional yet somehow the dark wood of the warehouse remained in shadow. It was as if the laws of physics didn't apply here and this building was immune to such silly things at the direction of light. A black hole, that's what it reminded her of, a massive object that absorbed light rather than reflecting it.

As she got out of her car she reminded herself what the officer had said, *"I'm sorry, Mrs. O'Connell. That particular stretch of road sees about twenty five hundred vehicles a day. That's a lot of suspects, Mrs. O'Connell."*

Her disdain for the apparent pitiful work ethic of the modern police force had grown from non-existent to a burning rage in the last two weeks.

"We'll keep looking, Mrs. O'Connell. It'll be ok. You just go home and wait for our call. We have good people here, working night and day, Mrs. O'Connell."

There had been no call. No Updates, no progress, no hope. And then suddenly her phone lit up and it wasn't the police. Cheryl knew that she had no idea what to expect that night but her husband had laid there in that ditch for two days before he was discovered half eaten by the forces of nature. Whoever hurt Walter deserved whatever pain they had been through, she was sure of it. Terrifying as this place was, it was time to see for herself.

The knock on the large doors was spectacularly loud considering her small hands. Cheryl stood back as a series of locks snapped open and The Good Samaritan swung the massive entryway open. He was enormous, she thought, thank God she knew that he was on her side. She couldn't imagine encountering this man in a dark alley and being dragged into his nightmarish home.

The door slammed shut after she entered and the mysterious man led her down a long, dark hallway. The walls were lined with old mattresses which seemed bizarre and cracks in the wood allowed the street lights to leak through into the light deprived space. The man spoke to her as they walked, passing through the almost soothing streaks of light.

"This woman has confessed to your husband's murder." His voice was shockingly calm and even comforting. She marveled at what an intimidating sight he was but still somehow his voice offered a sense of warmth.

"She has been through every pain possible, I made sure of it. Her suffering has far exceeded that of your husbands. And she has truly repented. Now, it's time for her to live or die. But this is not my choice." He stopped and turned to her. "Only you can decide."

The Good Samaritan pushed open a set of swinging doors as if he were presenting The Greatest Show on Earth. Cheryl admired the massive interior room and its many layers of abandoned machines, dust and eventually a center stage of blood and pain. The stranger continued to lead her into the center of the room where, beneath a blinding spotlight, sat the star of the show.

A naked, shredded body was tied to a wooden chair. The battered form of Sloane Kelli was difficult to look at. Her skin had been torn and stapled back together. Puncture wounds of various sizes had been carefully placed in non-lethal areas and then stapled or burned. Cheryl didn't know if this woman had a full head of hair before arriving, but her scalp was thin at best. Had she encountered this body anywhere else, she would have assumed the time of death had been days before but this one was somehow still alive. Cheryl shuddered as she finished examining her husband's murderer.

"I'll give you a moment." said The Good Samaritan as he turned to exit the light.

"No." Cheryl's response stopped the man dead in his tracks. Something was different about this moment. As many times as he had done this, surprises were rare. Different results, sure, but certainly a limited number of predictable responses from those he helped. He turned and slowly returned to Cheryl.

"She's had enough," she clarified. His brow furrowed and he studied her face. Yes, the point of all of this was to give these victim's the choice but something was different about her voice. There was a confidence he had never heard before, not when someone was standing right before the physical embodiment of evil.

"She's a murderer, she deserves to go to jail. You said you'd do that, right? Make sure she goes to jail if that's what I wanted?"

He nodded slowly. This must always be an option, if not he knew that he risked becoming a madman. The Choice mattered more than anything and many before had chosen clemency. While he knew that the freedom of a prison cell would never be his choice for these monsters, he sometimes admired the remarkable compassion it took for victims to allow themselves to show mercy. There had even been a few that had not chosen to go to the police at all, trusting instead that the process itself had been enough. He did not care for this choice as it came with too great a risk. Evil is evil and will always repeat itself given the chance.

"Then do it," Cheryl proclaimed and she exited the room having passed down her judgment leaving The Good Samaritan and Sloane in the quiet room.

He turned to the bloodied woman with his jaw clenched. He knew that she would be tried not as a murderer but as a white female in America. He knew that women's prison did not come with the same inherent consequences of a men's prison. As he walked behind Sloane to cut her bonds, he was able to comfort himself by examining his work. It had been a thorough and effective process and the punishment that shel had been through was ten times what even the worst prison could offer.

That would have to be enough, he thought as his knife sliced through the thin ropes that had buried themselves into her skin. Sloane's barely breathing body began to lean to one side and she slowly slid off the chair and hit the wooden floor with a thud. The Good Samaritan grabbed her ankle and dragged her body towards the exit. It was time to prepare another package for the grateful members of the city police department.

———

The window unit purred a comforting and steady sound, ushering in a cool breeze that the warm city refused even at night. Corbin stood at the doorway to Jean and Bella's bedroom, glad that they had comfortable beds to sleep in. At least he had been able to give them that.

There really was something truly remarkable, he thought, about a child sleeping. Their soft breaths and relaxed eyes were almost like a spell that you couldn't look away from. In a world filled with chaos and pain, it was easier to forget about it for these brief moments. In Bella's case, it was nice to see her sit still for the first time in the day. Corbin checked the time on his phone and left the room.

In the living room, Mrs. Livingston was settling into the reclining chair, readying herself for an evening of late night television. She was an elderly woman, Corbin assumed at least seventy five, sporting a classic grandmother look complete with the pale skin and thin glasses that rested on her nose. She had a slight accent he had never been able to place but she had been stateside for so long that it had all but faded.

Until recently Corbin had been sure that Mrs. Livingston did not care for his presence in the building. He had always hoped that it was not due to the color of his skin but perhaps some sort of misunderstanding about the unusual hours he kept. Regardless, as soon as two precious little girls started coming by more frequently, she was filled with smiles and regard. Corbin had cautiously asked if baby sitting would be an option on nights like this one and he was pleasantly surprised when she kissed him on the cheek in gratitude. There must not be many grandkids in the city for her.

"I can't thank you enough, Mrs. Livingston." Corbin checked his regular routine of items: gun, wallet, keys, phone.

"Not at all, you take your time," she responded with a smile. "I'll be asleep in no time, I'm sure."

It was nice to be friendly with someone in the building. That had never been a priority for Corbin. He opened his door and turned back to his new found friend.

"Don't invite any boyfriends over now," he said with a grin.

Nope, he thought as she shot a disapproving look at him. He broke eye contact with her and quickly nodded goodbye as he closed the door. He stepped down the old wooden stairs quickly with his hands in his pockets, making a mental note that funny is possibly not Mrs. Livingston's thing.

Driving through downtown at night was always peaceful, the bars and restaurants all having firmly rooted themselves into the Heights district just north. Corbin often thought that the late night arrivals at the precinct felt like the drive to catch an early flight before the rest of the world started their day. Something about the privacy of the experience made it feel like a privilege he was lucky enough to do.

With so little activity, any other vehicles stood out like a red head in Japan. As Corbin approached the station, he noticed the reflection of brake lights flash across the windows and immediately recognized it as cause for alarm. He rounded the corner to catch the silhouette of a sedan type vehicle whip around the block and out of view. To the right, on the sidewalk in front of precinct twenty three, a body had just come to rest.

"Holy shit!" Corbin sped up then quickly squealed to a halt in front of the station. He flew from his vehicle, putting his phone to his ear. He called for medical assistance as he examined the body and found that she was alive.

He hesitated to look at the woman at all at first, she had been beaten and ripped to shreds on nearly every part of her skin. Her naked body was twisted from broken bones in her right arm and left leg. Strapped by a zip tie to her left wrist was a plastic bag the contents of which Corbin already knew before he opened it. It would be filled with incriminating evidence that proved some horrible crime this person had committed. Evidence that could have been used to punish her legally. Christ, he thought, if only this psychopath had decided to become a private detective all of this would be a lot easier.

The ambulance arrived quickly and Corbin climbed in with the victim, silently hoping that his car wouldn't be towed from the highly illegal space he had parked it. The technicians rushed to set the woman's bones and strap down any loose limbs. They frantically searched for a source of bleeding to make sure she wouldn't bleed out but couldn't find a single injury that hadn't been completely sealed. The fall to the sidewalk had given her a fresh scrape to the forehead which the EMT's dutifully patched with a Band-Aid.

As they continued to examine the victim and keep a sharp eye on her vitals, which were stable but very close to death, Corbin opened the bag. There was never any particular system involved with the evidence provided, Corbin had always gotten the distinct feeling of disdain when sorting through these bags. It was as if The Good Samaritan felt that he had done enough for the police and that they should be made to organize the paperwork themselves as it was not in his job description.

Before long Corbin was able to find the name Sloane Kelli and told the EMTs just in case she regained consciousness. Upon further reading, it became clear that this woman had been involved in the death of the cyclist who had been found in a ditch near county road four eighty six. Corbin didn't need to read any further just yet, he knew how the rest of the story would play out. He would comb through the information, hoping to find a mistake and eventually agree that the victim was guilty.

While all of the information was new to him, he found himself questioning whether this woman deserved such a punishment after a hit and run. So many of the victims had committed truly evil crimes, an accident like this one was typically a tragedy of unfortunate events and purely circumstantial. What would possess a man to pursue this level of violence over something that was unintentional? Corbin hoped that the victim being a woman was not influencing his feelings of sympathy but had to admit it was possible. There were a lot of details that would have to be examined before he could really understand.

This is going to be a long night, Corbin thought as he prayed for some extreme amenability from the sweet Mrs. Livingston.

Chapter 16

A rare breeze slid through the alley brushing Sarah's cheek as she passed. It was a frustrating icing on the cake Sarah had been given that day. She was not used to good days or uplifting outlooks and had learned to shut out the expectation of such things. This skill had been challenged during her shift as the customers all treated her with respect and tipped well, the commute was pleasant, Casey persisted in pursuing her but it annoyed her less and now even the fucking breeze was on her side.

"God damn it," she said out loud as she fruitlessly brushed the breeze from her face. When she was a teenager she had been told by the DCF therapists about her wall that she had built but she preferred to think of it as a suit of armor. Her protective coating of anger and solitude kept her safe. She had been weak once, she had been a victim once. Never again.

Sarah quickened her pace as her thrift store hiking boots turned the corner to her block. Just a few more steps and she would be tucked within the safe haven she had built for herself. Once there, maybe she would allow herself to appreciate the day and even consider being grateful for it. The foyer door always jammed and she thrusted her shoulder into it just enough to be granted access.

Sarah lived on the fifth floor, a level that she was always happy with for reasons she had never really put a label on. Something about it was high enough to feel safe from the ground level and also provide a modest view of the surrounding area. As she approached the fourth landing she took note that she was not alone. The wooden steps led to four apartments on each floor. Just in front of apartment 4B, a little girl sat on the hard wood holding her knees to her chest. They made eye contact as Sarah stepped onto the landing.

The girl had dirty blonde hair and fair skin peppered with a tremendous amount of freckles. She looked to be about nine years old and wore a hand-me-down t-shirt and jean shorts. The two broke eye contact almost as soon as they had made it but the damage had been done. Sarah saw the cut on her lip before the little girl had been able to hide it.

Sarah stared at the floor, frozen in uncertainty. A tidal wave of images flooded her mind as she fought back all the memories that had been buried. It was too recently that she had sat outside her own front door with her own wounds. Sarah remembered her armor.

Quickly, she continued her ascension of the stairs, passing by the little girl as she stepped onto the flight that led to the fifth floor. Halfway up the steps she heard the door to 4B open and she slowed to a stop. Trembling, Sarah turned to see who had broken the silence. To her horror, she saw that her father had stepped outside the door and shot a vicious glare up at her that made her freeze in place. She closed her eyes.

No. He's dead. He's gone.

She opened her eyes again and saw a man she didn't recognize. The brown haired, beer bellied figure looked to be just past forty. He wore some sort of uniform pants and an undershirt that needed a good washing. Sarah was unable to release her gaze at the man but he hadn't yet noticed her.

The little girl's father did not look at her as he spoke calmly down at her, "Caitlin. Get up. Inside."

It was cold, unfamiliar. Caitlin stood without responding or making eye contact with her father and stepped into the apartment making sure to take another look at Sarah who was still staring at the large man. Sarah's heart was racing so fast that it hurt, her breathing had quickened but she was forcing her chest to restrict itself to stay as quiet as possible. Still unable to move her feet, she could only hope to remain invisible.

Caitlin's father finally turned to follow his daughter and caught a glimpse of the strange girl on the stairs beside him. They locked eyes and Sarah's armor fell to pieces. Tears formed in her eyes yet she remained perfectly still. The man studied her for a moment, then stepped inside with a feeling of bewilderment after such a strange encounter.

As soon as the door latched, Sarah bolted up the stairs. She fumbled with her keys and jammed them into the deadbolt as if she were being chased. Slamming and locking the door behind her, she rushed immediately to the kitchen where she could set herself in her perch at the window sill and all would be well. She didn't make it.

Just in time, she clung to the sink as she vomited what little she had eaten that day. It stung her throat and squeezed her chest so hard that she felt like she was choking. A moment later she realized she was, in fact, choking and she fell to the floor taking a dish towel with her that brought a collection of plates and pans to the ground. The plates shattered and the pans rang through the small apartment as she collapsed. The suffocating sensation passed as she finally gasped for air.

There, on the kitchen floor of apartment 5B, Sarah wrapped herself into a ball as she sobbed. She hadn't cried like this in nearly a decade and it felt like a dam had been released. She felt as though her body couldn't physically provide the tears that were needed, she wailed in agony as much as she could until her voice left her and she could only breathe and whisper.

"Help me.....oh my god, help me."

Sarah had not taken a full breath in over ten minutes and she began to feel light headed. She felt herself leave her body and float to the ceiling. From there, she looked down at herself bleeding and crying on her childhood bedroom floor. Daddy had just left and the pain was still fresh. It always faded eventually but in the moments immediately following one of his visits she could almost feel the outline of his fist on her body and the radiating sensation stung well after he left.

That poor, scared little girl, she thought. She looks so alone. Sarah floated back into herself and felt her eyelids grow heavy. She remained on the cracked tile until her eyes closed, bringing an odd sense of quiet and peace in the space that she would not get to enjoy. That night, Sarah's mind would find no peace and her dreams would be filled with terror.

———

The wounds on Sloane Kelli's body had been properly stitched, her skin had been washed of the dried blood and her head had been shaved in order to access the many wounds across her scalp. When she had first awoken in the hospital her initial panic was caused by the foreign sensation of having no depth perception due to the loss of her left eye. The staff had calmed her down and she quickly set out to adjust to her new way of looking at the world.

Her husband, Richard, had not been to see her yet. Sloane looked at the clock one more time, she had been conscious for three hours and had asked for him right away. Outside her room a uniformed police officer stood watch, she was afraid to speak to him, unsure if she was considered a victim or a criminal.

Sloane slowly lifted the covers and pushed her gown to the side, revealing her body. She had been waiting for Richard to check on the full extent of her injuries so that he could be there for support but that seemed to be wishful thinking at this point. She shuddered upon surveying the collection of bruises and stitches that covered her from head to toe. Truly, she thought, she looked like Frankenstein's monster and always would. She replaced the covers and sat back.

The broken woman shed a single tear and surprised herself when she breathed a sigh of relief. She had been punished and she had gotten what she deserved. Her future scars would serve as a reminder of what she had done until the day she died which was a merciful sentence.

Suddenly there was movement outside the door and she sat up in anticipation of Richard's arrival. But it wasn't him, rather it was a man in a suit who entered the room. He was a handsome man with a look of exhaustion on his face.

"Good Morning," he said. "I'm John Corbin. We had the pleasure of meeting last night but you were taking a nap at the time. How are you feeling?"

Sloane was slow to respond, still unsure who she was in this room, unsure what the people around her thought of her. "I'm ok. Mostly everything's numb. Are you a cop?"

"Detective. Yes." he said as he sat down on a chair beside her bed. "I have some questions for you if that's alright."

"Why are you being so nice to me?"

Corbin looked at her for a moment before answering. Once again, the trademark influence of this killer was revealing itself. "Innocent until proven guilty, I suppose."

"I am guilty. There's no innocence." she said with a touch of judgment in her voice as if to criticize this officer of the law for not treating her like a criminal.

"Well, be that as it may. We still have a job to do. If you are tried and convicted, then you will be guilty as far as the state is concerned."

"So what happens next?"

"That depends. What can you tell us about him?"

She turned her head to stare at the ceiling, her one good eye studying the bright LED lights above her. She hadn't considered this, the idea that somehow this process would include proving the guilt of anyone but herself. She alone had done what she did, it was only Sloane Kelli who hid the evidence and set out to move on with her life as if nothing had happened. She had killed a man. She had widowed a young woman. Her lip quivered as she remembered the words she heard The Good Samaritan whisper to her just before he tossed her to the concrete, she had also been responsible for the loss of the poor woman's child.

What can you tell us about him? The words echoed in her head. As much as the stranger had been her kidnapper and her tormentor, he was her savior. Had it not been for him, she would have never admitted to her crime and her soul would have eaten itself until the end of her days. She now felt a freedom that had come at a very severe price, but it was freedom nonetheless.

"You can make a deal with the state attorney. This case matters to them. If you can help us find him you could be looking at less time." Corbin offered.

"I don't want less time," she snapped back.

Corbin was frustrated but not entirely surprised. This was typical of most of these victims, Warren being the exception. "If you're planning on pleading guilty, I'll need a full account of what happened to you. Including how you wound up on the steps of a police station."

"It won't help you. He's not an idiot. He wouldn't risk me knowing anything that would lead you to him."

"I'll take my chances," he said as he placed a digital audio recorder on her side table. "I know that you've been read your rights but I'd like to remind you that you have the right to an attorney before we have this conversation."

She shook her head, having already committed to pleading guilty. She thought for a moment, debating whether she would cooperate with the detective. It couldn't hurt, she decided, to tell her story. There was no absolution for her, she knew that, but she had experienced so much in the last few days that she had to admit it was hard to keep it quiet.

"He never said a lot, but I can't get his voice out of my head. I thought that after a while, I'd get used to the pain. But every time he cut me, it felt like the first time. He said he found me."

She thought back to that day The Good Samaritan caught her scent downtown. At the time she hadn't noticed him but in the time since she had remembered flashes of images from the corner of her eye.

"He said he has a gift. He can see straight through people. When they're in pain. When they've hurt someone." A tear slid down her cheek. "He could see the guilt in my eyes even in just that brief moment. Then he found me. And he took me...there."

"Where is 'there'?" Corbin asked.

She turned to him with a smirk, "You don't really think I know that do you? Like I said, he's too smart for that." She resumed staring at the lights. By now the brightness was uncomfortable on her eyes, a sensation that she found oddly comforting.

Her voice broke slightly as she continued, "He kept staring at me. With those eyes. Kept ... watching the blood escape my body. Like I was a piece of art, and he was deciding where his next stroke would be."

"Sloane," she turned to the detective as he spoke. "I need to find this man."

"I know," she spoke to him as if she were the enlightened one and he had yet to even become a student. "But you won't. And I won't help you. Even if I did tell you anything that would give what you need, I'd rather die in prison than go back there. He'd find me. Anywhere."

Corbin saw the finality in her eyes and he knew this conversation was over. There would be time in the future to try again but he knew how that would go as well. He stood and left the room, leaving Sloane with the new found comfort of knowing that she was, in fact, the criminal and not the victim.

The Good Samaritan sat on a bench at the edge of Fulton Park with a newspaper spread across his lap. He had always preferred the texture of the printed news even as digital media took over worldwide. There was a certain class lent to a story being told on these pages, similar to the organic feel of thirty five millimeter film as compared to today's digital cameras. He didn't have much interest in modern politics or even very much of what was happening in local events but occasionally the press would share a story about one of his adjudicated souls. Obviously the police kept some information to themselves but it was helpful to know what they were sharing with the press. On a few occasions, a tragic story about a crime with no suspects had led him to his next student.

Across the street from the park was a neighborhood that once was full of color. It wasn't thirty years ago that the area had been a cultural center filled with music and festivals. Some of the best restaurants in the city had survived the decades of decline and were now starting to close their doors. It was no longer safe to be on these streets after dark, even the taxis would take the long way around just to be sure their passengers would stay safe.

Sarah's story about the store being robbed on a regular basis was not surprising, that sort of thing happened even in the nicer parts of town. To him, she was a pest but he had to admit that his own impulses made it near impossible to be aware of acts of injustice and do nothing. A convenience store getting knocked over every once in a while was not a major concern of his but with Sloane resting comfortably at Saint Mary's he had time on his hands.

In fact, Sloane had made today's paper. The police declined to share any information at this point which made the story of little interest. However, apparently dear Richard had chosen to distance himself from his criminal wife, having been quoted claiming that he had no idea she had done such a terrible thing. The Good Samaritan made a note of that.

The story went into further detail about the extent of the woman's injuries and where she had been discovered by one Detective John Corbin. This was not a new name, he had been mentioned in many of the articles over the last few years. The Good Samaritan allowed a small smile at the thought of the headlines on the day that the press finally connected her to the hit and run they had already covered in depth.

Across the street the small bell above the Lucky Saver main entrance rang out. The Good Samaritan watched as two young men entered and began to shop, the man behind the counter took interest in their presence and seemed concerned. He stood and crossed the street as the young criminals began shouting at the man to empty his register using profanity and racial slurs. In the coming days it would be a few simple searches online to learn the identities of the young men in order to keep track of them. Anthony and Jose had been repeating this habit for months, already choosing a life of hurting others at the young ages of nineteen and twenty.

Anthony held his gun up to the store owner at a ninety degree angle, presumably he had seen that in a movie and thought it looked cool despite how much it would reduce his accuracy if he were to actually take a shot. The old man finished sliding the cash into a brown paper bag and put it on the counter.

"Have a nice day, bitch," taunted Anthony as he and Jose exited the store with smiles on their faces.

The store owner quickly locked the door behind them and exhaled a sigh of relief. Anxious to get home and count the spoils of their conquest, the young men rounded the first corner into an alley. With incredible strength The Good Samaritan's arm reached out from the shadows and grabbed Anthony by the jacket, swinging him headfirst into the brick wall and he fell to the floor unconscious. Jose clumsily reached for a gun that he had not pulled out in the store, as he raised it to aim at his assailant, the man from the shadows grabbed his wrist and snapped it back. The gun dropped and The Good Samaritan used his other hand to force Jose to the ground.

A heavy hand pushed down on Jose's chest, further restricting his breathing after already having the wind knocked out of him. As he gasped for breath he looked up and saw only shadows except for an eerie brightness that shined from piercing blue eyes. The Good Samaritan moved his hand from Jose's wrist and pulled a small knife from behind him. The knife slid quickly into Jose's knee, he tried to cry out in pain but his chest wouldn't allow it. The Good Samaritan grabbed his neck and squeezed as he lifted.

"Leave this man alone," he whispered.

Jose frantically nodded his head as tears leaked onto his cheeks then his eyes shifted as he noticed Anthony begin to sit up. The Good Samaritan turned, removed the knife from Jose's knee and threw it into Anthony's shoulder. Both men cried out in pain. The man in shadow stood and removed the knife from Anthony's shoulder before quietly and calmly exiting the alley. It would be important to follow up with his new students, but this was a good first lesson.

Chapter 17

Three men stood before the towering entrance of a warehouse that dated back at least a hundred years. Detectives John Corbin and Victor Jackson had been waiting patiently for the arrival of Louis Hernandez, the owner, for more than thirty minutes. When he finally arrived he offered no apologies but gave them the opportunity to thank him for sparing his precious time.

Finding Mr. Hernandez was something of an adventure in itself. With only days left to close this case, Corbin began cold calling real estate agents and property brokers in an attempt to establish just how many warehouses within the city limits there were and how many of them were vacant. The generic description of the interior of an old factory was not much to go on but the search eventually led him to a forgotten part of town.

The city set down its roots when industry was booming and thanks to a select group of immigrants, cigars became what would help this town make its name. He had always heard that but never bothered to learn more. If he had he might have known that just outside of downtown was a decent collection of warehouses that hadn't been used since the nineteen fifties. The process of searching them started with scouring the city's records one at a time to see who the current owners were.

Corbin had scheduled this meeting with Mr. Hernandez with the understanding that whoever showed up for the meeting could very well be the man that the media had labeled "The Good Samaritan" and he was prepared to make an arrest. When the old man arrived sporting gym shorts and a guayabera style shirt and standing a solid five foot four inches above the ground he set his mind at ease. Mr. Hernandez opened the door with a set of keys that had not been updated in the last seventy-five years and pushed the large doors open.

As the detectives walked the halls of the dusty old building they could not have known they were walking in a near clone of the one they were searching for. The walls were empty and the floor hadn't been walked on by anybody but dear old Louis in some time. It was hot beyond belief as the sun baked the tin roof and snuck in through the cracks in the walls. Central air conditioning had not even been dreamed of when this structure was built and Corbin was beginning to understand how a place like this would make the perfect location to mentally dismantle a human being.

"How many of these do you own?" Jackson asked Mr. Hernandez. Corbin already knew that answer and continued studying the rooms they were passing as they continued down the corridor.

"Just this one and the one next door," Mr. Hernandez explained. "They ain't expensive to buy, but rather it be me buyin' 'em 'stead of some government pricks comin' to tear 'em down. Pieces of history, these buildings are! The whole God-damned foundation of this city is in these warehouses, you know?"

"No I didn't know that," said Jackson genuinely.

"Are you the only one with keys to the building?" Corbin spoke up.

"Damn right. Don't trust nobody but me, Louis K. Hernandez." He beat his chest in case they had forgotten who he was talking about. "That's the only way to survive in this day and age. It used to be about havin' guts and bein' a man. Now, all you need is some sleazy lawyer. Crooked government pricks."

Corbin had taken care of his grandmother as a teenager. She suffered from a form of dementia he was too young to understand or care about, his responsibilities were a chore rather than done out of love. During that time he grew to understand the times in which you need to begin ignoring the ramblings of the elderly. This conversation was quickly beginning to feel familiar and he chose to remove himself from it as he entered into the main production floor.

The room was massive and reached at least forty feet high. There were no windows and steel columns were posted every fifteen feet on either side of the space. The area was empty for the most part aside from a few old cars and about thirty years of dust.

"Jackson, take pictures just in case. We'll show them to Warren and see if they ring a bell." Corbin commanded.

Jackson listened dutifully and began snapping photos with his phone at all angles.

"What are ya tryin' to find anyhow?" Mr. Hernandez pried.

"Oh, just a routine investigation," Jackson said with a smile. "We're checking out all the unused warehouses in the area."

"All of 'em?" Mr. Hernandez seemed impressed.

"Yes sir." Jackson replied.

"Well, I hope you boys got a lot of time on your hands."

Corbin turned. "Why do you say that, Louis?"

Mr. Hernandez chuckled lightly, "Well, you got two dozen of 'em in this district alone."

He left the main production floor suddenly, expecting the detectives to follow. They looked at each other and decided it was best to see where he was headed. They pushed through the swinging doors and followed the old man into one of the side rooms with a window. He pointed outside towards an impressive display. Dozens of warehouses lined the streets, relics of an era long since past. Each one was nearly identical, having been built to serve the exact same purpose.

"Every one of them things is unused." Mr. Hernandez explained. "Them owners haven't sold yet, neither. Holding out, just like me. Crooked government pricks."

Corbin's heart sank. He knew the area was large but had no idea each and every building was potentially suspect. He knew right away that he would never be able to authorize the manpower needed to inspect these properties in the time allowed, not to mention the incredibly daunting task of getting warrants for each of them and time was running short. He checked his watch and shot a look at his partner.

"Shit. Jackson, we got to go," he said as they rushed out of the room, thanking the old man for his time on the way out. Mr. Hernandez remained alone in the quiet building, happy to have been a part of something exciting.

———

A small group of officers surrounded Warren Sheffield and he prepared himself for what he considered to be the bravest things he'd ever done. In just a moment he would step out of the wooden doors ahead of him and announce to the world that he was a victim of The Good Samaritan. He knew doing so was almost certainly signing his own death certificate but for the sake of justice he felt it was the right thing to do, no matter what happened to him.

Detectives Corbin and Jackson shook hands with Jerry Smith as he approached the group. Jerry was a man of average height, a thinning hairline and wore round framed glasses that reminded Warren of Harry Potter as he stepped forward. Jerry was a public information officer, meaning that it was his job to share curated information about active police investigations with the press, or acting as the condom between the police and the press as he liked to phrase it at cocktail parties. Catching the press up on the details of the history of this particular series of murders had become somewhat routine with the crimes being so repetitive and him being able to share so little information. It had become a chore, but at least this time things were shaken up a little bit and he was honestly curious to see what would come next.

"It's three thirty. Are you ready?" Corbin asked as he put his hand on Warren's shoulder.

Warren's chubby cheeks shook as he nervously nodded 'yes' and the doors swung open. Outside a small crowd had gathered, consisting mostly of reporters and their camera operators but with a few members of the public scattered throughout. Each station had placed their own microphone with their logos prominently featured on the podium that stood between the officers and the crowd. The crew readied themselves and checked the settings on their cameras.

"Hello everyone," Jerry said as he approached the podium. "Are we all set? Everyone ready? Ok. Hello, I'm public information officer Jerry Smith. Behind me is Homicide Detective John Corbin, C-O-R-B-I-N, he is leading the investigation of this particular crime series. And also behind me is Warren Sheffield, S-H-E-F-F-I-E-L-D, a victim, and he will be making a statement today."

Jerry paused for a moment to allow some of the people in attendance to write the information down. Print media was not entirely dead and there were still a few analogue soldiers that did things the old fashioned way.

"Ok," he continued as he read from a printed statement in his hands. "Over the past several years, there have been a series of murders with strikingly similar characteristics, many details of which we cannot reveal at this time. They appear to have all been committed by one man who has been described as over 6 feet tall, blonde hair, blue eyes, medium build. There seem to be many witnesses, though only a handful have come forward with their testimony. The purpose of today's conference is to attempt to encourage those witnesses to come forward and help us make sure this suspect is apprehended and tried by a jury of his peers. I will now turn the podium over to Mr. Sheffield."

Jerry vacated his space in the spotlight and extended his hand in an offer for Warren to step up. Warren cautiously obliged, his hands shaking as he pulled a crumpled piece of paper out of his pocket. Corbin had prepared a brief statement for him, 'Just read it and walk away' he had said. Just walk away. Warren placed the paper on the podium and lowered himself to the microphones, Jerry was considerably shorter than him. Warren noticed several faces in the crowd grimace at the sight of his disfigured face.

"Um .. Hi. I am one of many victims of the man we are trying to find," he read in a monotone, nervous voice like a fourth grader asked to read in front of the class. "So far, I am the only survivor of this man's crimes to speak up, I would like to encourage others in my position to do the same."

Warren looked up, finally removing his eyes from the paper. Suddenly an odd confidence struck him and he pushed aside the paper, now seeing it as a crutch.

"Um ... I can't really describe to you what I've been through," he began to shudder through his words. "He...tortures his victims for days. Weeks. I have very little feeling left in my feet as well as several other parts of my body. I don't sleep at night, food has no taste. And I live in constant fear that one day he will return for me. He forced my son to watch this. And I can see it in his eyes that he will never forget."

Jerry gently leaned over and tapped Warren on the shoulder who waved his hand as an apology. He pulled the printed sheet back to his eye line.

"If you know anyone who has been through what I have," he continued, "please encourage them to come forward. The more the police know about this man, the quicker we can bring him to justice."

That was it. 'Just walk away.' Warren folded the paper and stuffed it into his pocket as he turned to head inside. The press erupted with questions, all irritated that this conference was apparently not going to include a question and answer session. A young reporter from a local blog shoved her way to the front of the crowd with her phone aimed at the podium.

"Warren, what did you do?!" the eager reporter shouted.

The other reporters fell silent, impressed at not only the volume that came from such a small person but at the direct-ness of her question which they had all been thinking but been unwilling to say. The words felt like crashing cymbals in Warren's ears, he turned and locked eyes with her.

"What?" the word faintly slipped out of his mouth.

She stood up straight with confidence, "Well, everyone did something, right? I mean, The Good Samaritan doesn't just kill people for no reason, what was yours?"

The question was met with mixed reactions from the crowd, making a clear statement about the divisiveness of the issue. Corbin looked around at the collage of opinions on people's faces both for and against the arrest of this man. It was a comfort to him knowing for sure that he wasn't the only one there trying to do the right thing.

Warren considered answering the question for a moment but then quickly turned to hide within his police escort and they entered the building. Corbin took one last look at the crowd and stopped himself. A familiar face. A young woman stood in the crowd with a hat on, she was beautiful but looked unhealthy. She stared directly at him as if she knew him personally and broke her gaze once he met hers.

Corbin's mind raced through years of folders, crime scene photos and witness statements and then he had it. Years ago, well before he joined the case. Sarah Thompson. Her father had been killed and she was orphaned. His eyes widened with interest. Sarah turned her head once more to see if Corbin had moved on and upon realizing she had been recognized she turned and pushed her way through the crowd.

"Jackson!" Corbin was already running as he called out to his partner. Jackson dutifully followed suit, not yet knowing what he was running after.

The lunch time crowds of downtown were only just beginning to disperse as Sarah flew past restaurants and shops. Her pursuers followed as closely as they could but she was surprisingly fast for someone who seemingly made little effort to take care of herself.

Corbin removed a handheld radio from his belt as he shouted at pedestrians in his way, "Move! Move! Unit one fifteen to dispatch."

A crackled voice responded quickly, "One fifteen, go ahead."

"In pursuit of suspect on foot. Female. Caucasian. Early twenties, wearing blue jeans and a black hat. Requesting backup. Headed south on Madison at York." It had never occurred to him how difficult talking and running at the same time was and he found himself disappointingly exhausted at the end of his sentence.

"Ten-four one fifteen, backup is on its way." the voice confirmed.

The detectives rounded another corner and began to close in on their prey. Sarah noticed they were close and began toppling chairs and tables to slow them down. The obstructions were easy enough to jump over and Corbin was glad to see that her efforts only decreased their distance.

Sarah turned another corner and was met by a squad car squealing to a stop, she immediately changed directions and crossed the street. She entered an alley and darted straight for a fire escape that was just low enough for her to reach. Upper body strength was never her finest quality, she reminded herself as she tried to lift her full weight up onto the ladder when suddenly she felt a strong hand wrap around her ankle.

Corbin pulled the suspect off the ladder and she fell to the ground, her head slamming into a dumpster on the way. Sarah lay on the wet brick, her forehead slowly bleeding from the impact, unconscious.

"Shit," Corbin muttered when he saw her injury.

Jackson finally caught up with his partner and took a brief moment to survey the situation. "'Cuff her," Corbin commanded as he tried to catch his breath. The two men waited for a squad car to arrive so they could bring their prize back to the station for questioning.

Warren's police escort arrived at his house just a few seconds before he did and he slowly passed them to pull into his own driveway. Before turning off the ignition, Warren examined his front yard and what he could see of the sides of the house. Satisfied that he would be safe, he pulled his keys and stepped towards his front door. The officers in the patrol car ignored his friendly wave as they put their vehicle into park and settled in to begin their long night of babysitting. The two men had differences of opinion as far as what should be done about this killer but they were both mutually irritated by the order to watch over a rapist or murderer or whatever this creep was.

The house was modest but in a nice enough neighborhood, Warren had managed to get a good deal when the market was in his favor. His wife had left eleven years ago leaving him with the payments which he had barely been able to maintain. The house and most of its contents reminded him of a life that once was better.

Warren kicked off his shoes and loosened his tie as he sank into his favorite recliner. Today wasn't physically exhausting but the emotional toll of inviting death to his door was a heavy burden to bear.

"Kyle! Where you at?" Warren shouted with his eyes shut.

His son opened his bedroom door and stood in the doorway to the living room. Kyle was small for his age, often mistaken for being nine or ten. His brown hair was a mushroom cut style, calling back to the nineties when he always felt he should have been born. Kyle's blue-green eyes looked at his father with general curiosity. He knew what Warren had done that day, he watched it live on the news.

Somehow, his father had not deemed it necessary to ask him his opinion on this plan to go to the media. Kyle had been happy with the way things were ever since the stranger had shown up explaining where his missing father went. Warren abandoning him for days at a time had not been too unusual, except that he usually called to explain why, after a day or two. He had only been nine years old at the time but all he had to do was take the bus to school and eat what food there was in the house. Since then it had occurred to him that showing his father mercy when The Good Samaritan gave him the choice was possibly influenced by the fact that the food had run out and he didn't know if he would be able to feed himself much longer.

When they returned home, Warren didn't look at his son for weeks. For a while it seemed that he was afraid of him, just as he feared The Good Samaritan. It took several months for the triggers to go away and the fight or flight responses to stop. But the beatings had ended. Warren didn't so much as touch his son anymore. Kyle even stopped making sure his father was always in front of him after a while, no longer fearing that a fist could be raised at any time.

Even two years later Warren walked around their home in a state of constant fear, seemingly always looking for a way to ease the anxiety. He had warmed up to his son slightly, attempting to build a father-son relationship that had never existed before.

"Hey," Warren said breathlessly. "Good day?"

"Yeah," his son replied. "Went over to Jake's. They had the news on."

Warren opened his eyes for the first time, he wasn't sure how to feel about this. Kyle could have responded any number of ways to seeing that press conference.

"Oh yeah?" he responded nervously. "What'd you think?"

"Tie made you look stiff. But it was fine."

"Thanks," Warren allowed a small smile. "I was pretty nervous."

"Why didn't you tell me?"

Warren looked at his son as though he had been caught red handed, unsure of what to say. Kyle turned and left the room for the kitchen again before Warren could think of anything, removing the trash bag and stepping out the back door. Warren sat in his comfortable chair wondering what he should have said in that moment and whether or not he would get a second chance.

Outside, Kyle lifted the large plastic lid and tossed the trash bag in, when the lid closed the intimidating silhouette of The Good Samaritan stood behind it. Kyle took a sharp breath in shock but immediately knew he was not in danger. This man had saved him and despite his murderous line of work and towering physique, he was a hero to the boy.

"You're back?" Kyle asked with respect. The Good Samaritan answered only by stepping into the light. "Are you gonna kill him?"

He knew that his father had taken a serious risk today. Had he known about it he may have even tried to convince him not to, but the choice would have been hard to make. Kyle had grown up fast and was no stranger to moral ambiguities. The man shook his head 'no' as he turned to study Warren watching TV through the window.

"He's changed. I know you don't believe it, but you changed him," Kyle was surprised by his own tone, defending his beast of a father was not normal for him.

"No one changes," The Good Samaritan said quietly.

"Then why give us the choice?"

The Good Samaritan stood silent, knowing there was no good answer to that question. He contemplated his own motivations for a moment before breaking eye contact with the boy and turning back to the man inside.

"I'm fine now. He's still got his problems, but he's too scared to do anything. Okay? You took care of it. You don't need to be here. Jesus, if he saw you he'd probably die of a heart attack."

"What a shame that would be," The Good Samaritan whispered.

Kyle smirked at the comment. "You can go. It's ok."

The young man turned and went back inside, locking the back door as his father had taught him to. The Good Samaritan remained for a few more minutes to study the man who had once been in his care before slipping back into the shadows.

Chapter 18

Detective John Corbin rushed down the precinct hallway followed closely by Jackson. The young detective noticed that his senior partner was sporting a look he had never seen before; optimism. He was positively beaming.

"She knows something, I know she does," Corbin said to no one in particular. "Did you see these files? We've never had a break like this, not even with Warren."

It was refreshing for Jackson to see Corbin appear to look forward to the next step he was taking in this case. It had been an uphill battle with little to no support, even he had to admit he didn't always back up his partner in a private conversation with other officers. But he knew what this meant, a real witness with a real connection to the murders and leverage to use against her. The only thing missing was a little bow wrapped around Sarah Thompson.

"I told the Captain you had a suspect." Jackson offered.

Corbin stopped and turned to his partner, unable to resist a small smile. "What'd he say?"

"He told me to go fuck myself."

With that pleasant image fresh in his mind, Corbin opened the door to Interview Room 4, leaving Jackson in the hallway. Inside, Sarah sat in an aluminum chair with her head resting on an old wooden table that looked like it spent too many years on the showroom floor of a Salvation Army store. Her thin wrists were bruised from several hours of struggling to free herself despite being chained by steel handcuffs which now rested underneath her head. The room was uncomfortably plain, not as intimidating as she had expected but terribly bland; well lit by white light and just the table and two chairs.

Corbin took a seat in the chair opposite the sleeping detainee. He studied her hair that needed a wash badly, her clothes that were clean but older than she was, the wound on her forehead that had since been treated by the precinct medical staff.

"Sarah." He spoke quietly, not sure if she was actually asleep or just actively ignoring him.

"Sarah?" He tried again.

Still not getting the response he was after, Corbin reached his foot under the table and shoved her chair back, causing her head to slip off her hands and thump on the table. With a grimace she groggily lifted her head.

"Good Morning," he mocked.

"Fuck off," Sarah was quick to reply.

He smiled at the response. As he continued to speak, Corbin offered his most sincere tone to help her know he was on her side.

"I'll be honest with you, you're very important to me. Not to show my cards or anything. You know why?"

She rested her head back down on the table to make sure he knew that whatever speech he had prepared was of no interest to her.

"There are so many pieces to this puzzle of mine and frankly I've hardly found any of them. You're one more piece. Hell, I have a feeling you're one of those missing pieces that really connects everything. For three years I've been working on this case." He paused for a moment to reflect on the trueness of that sentence and how long it really felt and how many before him had failed.

"Three damn years without anything to show for it. Because this guy, whoever he is, is so good that he doesn't leave anything behind. And when one of his victims survives he scares them so bad that they never talk."

The word "victim" caused Sarah to lift her head and look him in the eyes for the first time. Corbin took a breath, surprised that her gaze was actually quite intimidating, despite her small frame and the position she was in.

"And victims families have somehow been talked into keeping quiet," he continued. "It's a dead end case, there's nowhere to go when no one will talk. But then you showed up."

He paused for a good long moment, taking care with his next words. "Who's your victim, Sarah?"

The question made her chest tighten but she resisted an emotional response.

"You use that word 'victim' like you know what it means," she replied with calm disdain. "Every single piece of shit that has died deserved what they got and then some."

Corbin's eyes lit up with excitement, that was practically a confession. He knew this was a golden opportunity but didn't think she would simply offer him everything he needed.

"How are you involved?" he asked greedily.

Sarah slumps into her chair slightly, "I'm not." The statement disappointed her to hear it said out loud. Corbin studied her face as her demeanor changed and decided to dig on that a little later.

"You've had quite a life, Sarah." Corbin opened a manilla folder filled with a large collection of freshly printed papers. The documents were neatly organized with paper clips and Post-It notes with years written on them.

Corbin was already familiar with the information before him but he slowly browsed through the papers as he spoke, "Parents divorced at age seven. Father went missing at age fourteen. Now, I have my own theory about what happened to your dad. Could you tell me what happened?"

"Couldn't say for sure, we weren't very close." She looked at him as if he were a stranger reading her diary.

"Taken in by child services," Corbin continued. "Foster home one, foster home two, three, four. Juvenile detention. And I don't see *any* tax returns."

He looked up at her. "Sarah, you have a history. One that allows us to keep you here for as long as we want until you feel like you'd like to share some information with me."

She stared at him with a stubborn silence, no longer interested in playing his game. He dropped his slight smile, knowing that she needed to be treated as the person she had chosen to be: an ally to the mass murderer he had been pursuing for years.

"What happened to your father? When child services brought you in, upon examination they said you had permanent scars from long term abuse." He knew what he was doing, opening the wounds of an abuse victim. It was despicable but it had to be done.

Her jaw clenched as he pushed harder, "Was your father a bad man? Did he need to be taken care of?" He leaned in and tilted his head in curiosity. "Did you enjoy watching him die?"

In a flash, Sarah relived the moment her father died. Her savior had called her to the warehouse where villains met their end. She felt so small compared to the massive size of the building as she approached. Inside, the air was so thick that she thought she could reach out and touch it. When she saw her father strapped to the chair it was the first time she could ever remember being in his presence and not being afraid. As the blood escaped the slit that had opened his throat and coated his chest, she felt her pain evaporate. She had been saved. She did, in fact, enjoy watching the life drain from his eyes.

Corbin had crossed a line. Sarah reached her handcuffed hands behind her head and grabbed the top of her chair. In a single swift move she lifted it over her head and leaned forward swinging the chair over her head and down onto Detective Corbin who had raised his arm to shield his head from the impact. The thin metal bent as it collided with his forearm, sending him crashing to the ground. Sarah remained on her side of the table with her feet spread, ready for a return assault.

The door to the interview room swung open without a knock and in stepped Alex Sommers. Sommers was lean and cold looking. He wore a navy blue three piece suit with pinstripes and a black tie. His thin lips let out a "tisk" when he saw the officer on the floor and the young woman with bound hands standing behind the table.

"You haven't been agitating my client, have you, Detective Corbin?"

Corbin's face was a mix of confusion and anger as he put together the story without context. Someone had seriously paid for this woman's attorney and now everything would fall apart. Not only that, it was a damn celebrity attorney that Corbin knew only by reputation.

"Unless you're charging her with something more impressive than resisting arrest, I would like to drive Sarah home," the attorney said with a quiet confidence.

"This woman has just assaulted a police officer," the detective said as he stood.

"Oh. That is a problem," Sommers admitted. "Well I suppose we can talk about that when we talk about that gash on her forehead. Yeah?"

Corbin turned to look again at the injury on Sarah's head which, admittedly, would not have happened without his help. He knew how easy it would be to twist it into an excessive force charge and did not offer a response.

Sarah stood in shock at what she was witnessing, she had never seen this man before and wasn't sure what her next move was. Her eyes darted between the two men as Corbin stepped back, gesturing for her to leave. Sarah cautiously stepped around the table and past the detective.

Neither Sarah nor her newly acquired attorney said a word as they passed through the police precinct. Word had apparently spread about her presence and several officers took an interest in her appearance as she made her way past the rows of desks. Once outside, Sarah reached for a pack of cigarettes from the plastic bag of her belongings that had been handed to her on the way out.

"What was that about?" she asked as the butane flame lit her face in the evening light.

"I'm Alex Sommers. I'm an attorney."

"No shit, I watch the news. Who's paying for this?"

"A mutual friend," Sommers said without looking at her.

It didn't take Sarah long to figure out who he was referring to and when she did she felt embarrassed to not have thought of it sooner. She looked at the man with eagerness in her eyes.

"Are you serious? Why?" she asked.

He turned to her, "Apparently, it was very important to him that you spend as little time in jail as possible."

"How do you know him?"

Sommers made a point to ignore the question entirely and responded quickly. "Ms. Thompson, if you know my client as well as I assume you do, considering what he's doing for you, then you must know how important anonymity is to him. I have very few answers for you, and generally it seems like a good idea not to have many questions about him. Enjoy your freedom. Contact me if they give you any more trouble."

He handed her a business card that looked like it was worth more than her shoes and stepped into a small silver sports car parked along the curb. He sped off and left the released prisoner on her own once again. She stood in shock for a moment before beginning the long walk home.

———————

Sarah put her keys back into the plastic bag with the police department seal on it as she closed her door. She had never been much of a purse girl but the convenience provided by this temporary one had helped her to see the appeal. Before she stepped into her apartment, she paused to listen to the muffled sounds of an argument downstairs. It was not an unusual sound and had become a part of the daily soundtrack offered by living in her building.

She took another step inside and felt a presence she couldn't see or hear, but someone was there. Sarah turned and suddenly felt a powerful hand wrap around her neck and push her body into the wall, causing a picture frame to fall and shatter. The Good Samaritan leaned in, his sharp blue eyes burning into hers.

"I'm sorry. I am, I didn't mean to-"

He pushed on her neck harder and suddenly her airflow was cut off.

"I didn't tell them anything!" she pushed the words out. "I wouldn't... I wouldn't do that! It won't happen again. I swear!"

"Stay away." he growled.

The Good Samaritan waited another moment to watch her beg for air before he decided she had learned her lesson and he released her throat. She fell to her knees and gasped for air as she looked up at him with tears in her eyes. He stood over her, asserting his dominance.

"....I'm sorry," she whispered as she lowered her head and began to sob.

He turned and reached for the door, pausing for a moment to listen. The sounds of the argument downstairs that leaked through the cheap building materials. The Good Samaritan processed what he could hear and shrugged off the distraction before leaving the apartment.

The air outside was unusually cool, the pleasant breeze competed with the heat still radiating from the asphalt as The Good Samaritan approached his car. Just as he reached the driver's side, a crash and quiet scream came from the alley. Curious, he put his keys back into his pocket and approached the end of the corridor.

The shadows in this part of town were always especially dark, he easily slipped into hiding as he observed a man and a woman, about fifty feet away, being threatened by a thug with a knife. The mugger punched the man in the stomach which sent him to the ground in pain. The Good Samaritan could barely make out a quiet threat as the man grabbed the frightened woman and held the knife to her throat, she quickly dropped her purse as an offering.

Suddenly her husband jumped to his feet and tried to save his wife, the mugger was too quick and turned the knife on him. He shoved his blade into the man's stomach and quickly pulled it out to push it in once more where it remained, the woman's screams echoed through the city streets. The Good Samaritan studied the scene with apathy, remaining at the ready.

Standing over his victim's body, the mugger turned murderer looked first at his bloodied hands and then up at the remaining witness in a panic. Unsure of what to do, he searched the area for additional witnesses before she took the opportunity and ran in the opposite direction. The killer decided to cut his losses and collected the purse before fishing the man's wallet from his back pocket and removing the knife from his belly.

As the murderer passed the shadows at the end of the alley, The Good Samaritan extended his leg and pushed the man's back, sending him head first into the side of the black sedan. The dark stranger swiftly landed two hard blows to the head, popped the trunk and stuffed the limp body inside before quietly closing the lid. It had been unplanned but done efficiently. He picked up the purse and removed the woman's cell phone then dialed 9-1-1 before tossing the phone to the sidewalk. As he approached the driver's door, The Good Samaritan took a quick look around to make sure the street was clear of witnesses before getting in.

As the vehicle escaped into the night, the sobs of a newly widowed bride could be heard begging for help as she fled down the block.

Chapter 19

The hospital was always clean. Corbin appreciated that. As much as it was often quite a terrible experience to be within these walls, he had to admit that the space itself was really quite pleasant. He held Bella's hand as they stepped into the elevator, Jean took the responsibility of pressing the button for the third floor. She wasn't on her phone today, Corbin noted, another day of growing up beyond her years.

As they walked through the metal doors and down the long hallway to Rachel's room, he had to wonder if Jean was thinking the same thing that he was. There were a limited number of these visits and he knew it. One day they would get a call and then the bed at the end of this hall would be empty or already filled with the next person waiting for a miracle.

Bella rushed into Rachel's room as they rounded the corner but was careful not to jump onto her bed. Corbin breathed a sigh of relief when he saw that their mother was awake and ready for them, Jean walked in with a smile and both girls hugged Rachel with care. Corbin looked at his former wife, sad to see that she had deteriorated quite a bit since the last time they saw her.

As he listened to his daughter's catch their mother up on their lives, a wave of dark truth washed over him.

"...and then Brody said that we could go over to their house this weekend," said Bella.

It was scary to know that he would forever be expected to be a better man than he believed himself to be. Rachel had been his foundation, she was the entire support structure that kept these children alive, beautiful and strong.

"He did? Oh, that will be fun. Is Chelsea going to be there too?" Rachel responded with as much enthusiasm as she could muster.

What was worse was that he would be without his friend. Corbin knew they would have never gotten back together but the girls were a tether that ensured Rachel would always be in his life which was a great comfort to him even after everything.

"Yeah, we're gonna stay the night," Jean clarified.

"Ooh, a slumber party. Well I hope you have a good time. Make sure you stay up way too late," Rachel teased.

Corbin didn't know how long it would take but the end was close, he could see it. He could feel it, and so could Jean.

"Are you gonna get better soon?" Bella asked. "We want you to come home."

Rachel considered her answer before offering it, "Well, I don't know yet, sweety. The doctors took some tests today and tomorrow they're going to tell me how I'm doing."

"Do you need some medicine, mommy?" Bella studied the tubes running from her mother's arms up to the clear plastic bag hanging over her bed.

"Yeah, baby. They want to give me medicine. But they don't know just what yet kind I need." Rachel was finding it harder to hold back her tears. She turned to her ex-husband and begged him with her eyes.

He jumped and peered out the door into the hallway. "Uh, nurse?"

As she approached, he turned to the girls with his hands extended. "Hey, you guys want to go to the play room for a little while?"

Jean shot him a look and he pleaded with her, "Could you go with her, please?"

She reluctantly agreed and kissed her mother on the cheek before exiting. Once the room was cleared of children, Rachel allowed the tears to flow down her cheeks.

"The tests came back this morning," she said as she fumbled with a used tissue. "We're out of options."

Corbin had prepared a number of things to say when this time came. None of them were coming out. Nothing felt right.

"They said they can make me comfortable. But I won't last the week. That's what they said."

Corbin approached the bed and sat on the side, unable to look at her any longer.

"John," she spoke with a serious tone. "You have to take care of them."

He turned to face her as she broke into a sob, "You have to promise me that nothing will happen to them. You'll take care of them."

"I will," he finally responded. "I will."

Rachel pulled on his shirt to lift herself up and embraced the heart broken man. "Oh, God. Oh my God. I'm so sorry. I'm sorry, babies. I'm so sorry!"

Outside, a nurse sat at her station listening to the sounds of a mother knowing she would soon abandon her children. She had been caring for Rachel for some time and had gotten to know the girls. The heartbreak was very real for her as well.

"Rachel," Corbin whispered. "Give me your hands."

She remained upright and obeyed. They held hands and embraced a connection between them that had been lost. Together they prayed, not for a miracle but for peace and acceptance.

———

Routines can be comforting, healthy even. Regular routines and healthy habits can lead to better sleep, reduced anxiety and improved overall mental health. It occasionally occurred to The Good Samaritan that the repetitive nature of how he spent his time was becoming dull. This feeling was often washed away by the comforting sight of an evil person gaining an understanding of what was in store for them. One could taste the fear.

Brett McKinely never really had a fair shot at life. If he had had the education to express it he would have told people that he was the product of a capitalist society that failed him. The simple truth is that his father left, his mother was poor and nothing ever had any hope of getting better. When he was big enough to threaten an adult his family's poverty and the influences around him made it a foregone conclusion that he would enter a life of taking what others had in order to try to gain what little ground in life he could.

After four or five years of managing to stay out of prison, Brett had tried to earn his income through honest means and took various odd jobs, but in the end the easy money just made more sense. Muggings became his primary financial resource and for a time it kept food on the table and paid for his mother's medications. Suddenly, at the age of twenty five he found himself having been promoted from the modest title of street thug to murderer. It can probably be said that very few people ever intend to take another person's life and he was no exception.

But he had done it. Brett McKinely knew right away that his life was over when he pushed his blade into his victim's abdomen. He knew that justice would find him, but could never have guessed it would find him so quickly. It was actually very fitting that his unlucky life should lead to committing his first murder right in front of a notorious vigilante killer. Now The Good Samaritan stood before him on the main floor of the warehouse, Brett observed that all around him the floor had dark stains. He couldn't see very far past the center of the room due to the bright spot light above him. The circular light source surrounding the stained floor made the whole room look like a target, and he was dead center. Brett had been stripped down to his boxer briefs, his legs and hands were tied to the thick wooden chair.

The Good Samaritan towered over him, dressed in a black suit with no tie. Brett could see his cold blue eyes shine in the light before the rest of his face left the shadows. He had already been beaten severely and was bleeding through several small cuts on his body. The young thief turned murderer was not particularly intelligent but was smart enough to know that this was just the beginning. Much more was in store for him. He knew who this man was. The stories had been told for years especially among those who chose to live above the laws of society to earn their living.

At first, Brett hadn't been able to shake the almost starstruck feeling of realizing whose custody he was in but when the beatings began a hopeless reality set in; he was going to die. Not only would his life be over soon but it was going to be taken from him slowly and painfully. As The Good Samaritan kneeled before him, Brett remembered the words he had heard as he was being strapped to the chair.

I know you think you're sorry. I know you think you've learned your lesson.

Brett knew that he was not a murderer. He was a bad person, sure. But not a murderer. The stranger pulled a squeeze bottle out of a small black bag.

But the truth is you'll never know. Until you're damned to hell.

He wasn't a good person, Brett thought, but he could be. It wasn't his fault. The man squirted a clear liquid onto Brett's knee.

The problem is that I don't even know whether or not hell exists.

The liquid had a powerful odor. Brett looked at it, confused. The cold sensation was almost comforting in this sweltering place.

But, I'll do my best until you get there.

The Good Samaritan lit a match and dropped it onto Brett's knee which immediately burst into flames. The fire quickly spread down his leg to the floor but remained contained to just his left leg. Brett experienced a pain unlike anything he could have ever imagined, the screams that left his body sounded inhuman as they echoed through the wooden halls. An extreme panic set in as he violently thrashed as much as his bonds would allow, rocking the chair from side to side until it toppled to its side.

The impact added a new injury to Brett's head that The Good Samaritan had not intended but welcomed. However, the flames were now spreading to his other leg which was not on the schedule, so The Good Samaritan removed a bottle of vinegar from his bag and doused the flames with it. The added irritation to Brett's fresh burn wounds was too great for him to process, he wanted to pass out from the pain and couldn't believe he hadn't already.

Brett remained conscious. He was awake and completely present for each and every moment.

Days passed. Over time, Brett's screams turned into faint whimpers as his body's fight to produce enough blood began losing the race against the many wounds he received each day. No longer able to lift his head, when The Good Samaritan would enter the room there was almost no way to even respond with fear anymore. The fight or flight that had been instilled in him by thousands of years of evolution was now diminished to a slight increase in heart rate when the stranger would put his powerful hands on him.

At the beginning, Brett had been trying to keep track of the puncture wounds and likely broken bones but he had lost track by the end of the second day. He had come to welcome the continued torture having fully accepted his guilt. Evil people deserved to be punished and he knew that he was indeed an evil person. The Good Samaritan would preach to him as he sliced, snapped and punctured various parts of his body.

I wonder. If there is a hell, what is the devil like?

It was The Good Samaritan's words that would sink into Brett's mind and burn through his thoughts. They caused more pain than even his most vicious tools.

And what would he think of me?

Brett was sure he had little time left to live but if by some miracle he were to survive, he knew he would hear these words every night as he tried to sleep.

Would he hate me?

The seconds passed like hours. There seemed to be no end.

Would he see something of himself in me?

The Good Samaritan picked up a large hook that was attached to a rope and pulley reaching to the ceiling. The hook pierced through the meat between Brett's shoulder and neck like a tender steak and he was hoisted into the air, hanging just off the ground lifted only by his muscle tissue. Finally, The Good Samaritan thought, a real scream. Brett's cries of pain echoed through the room after so many quiet hours.

Or would he fear me?

There he remained, hanging in the balance between life and death.

Chapter 20

The view from the fifth floor fire escape was not exactly an ocean view but it had its perks. Snapshots of private lives were on display in the rows of windows that Sarah could see. She sat, resting on a blanket that would have been wrapped around her if it hadn't been so damn hot, smoking a cigarette in her adopted Mets t-shirt. The alley would sometimes act as a wind tunnel and the breeze could almost be called cool as it slid across her legs.

Tears soaked her pale cheeks. Sarah had spent plenty of time trying to figure out what it was about her protector that she was so obsessed with and the result was always embarrassingly empty. She hated the idea of being reduced to the stereotypical girl with daddy issues but had a hard time shaking the idea. And now she had failed him.

What was worse was that he didn't even want her around. The emotional impact of having failed something she was never asked to do was weighing heavily on her. Sarah felt stupid and ashamed as she repeated the events of that day in her head on a loop and lit a new cigarette.

The windows were active tonight. Across the alley, the building was a similar design as it was likely built at the same time but at some point it was acquired by a different owner. The resulting renovations led to a distinct difference in tenants, an upper and lower class. Sarah enjoyed getting brief glimpses into the lives of those who lived a little more freely than she did thanks to their position in life.

The view offered a story filled with colorful characters. On the fourth floor, two windows from the right, Work From Home spent most of his days ordering off Amazon and making every effort possible to stay inside. Third floor, 4 windows from the left, Cooks A Lot could always be counted on to over do her meals and Sarah often found herself jealous of the family that benefited from her culinary passion. Fifth floor, three windows from the right, Miss Nipples had long ago noticed Sarah's voyeuristic tendencies and had chosen not to care even when her gentlemen callers came to visit. It was a building filled with stories and life, looking at them now was an uplifting feeling that Sarah clung to.

Below her, Sarah heard the sound of a window opening followed quickly by the sounds of arguing which were silenced just as abruptly by the shutting of the window. She didn't look down but was immediately aware that her solitude had been spoiled. Panic set in, her safe space no longer safe.

"Hi," Caitlin said, peering up through the slats of the fire escape.

Sarah didn't respond and tried to convince herself that if she simply remained still the child would go away.

"You're Sarah, right?" Caitlin advanced up the stairs to the landing between their floors. Sarah sucked on her cigarette once again.

"I'm Caitlin." The little girl had stepped closer and extended her hand. Sarah couldn't resist turning to her and acknowledging her outstretched hand which seemed like an odd thing for such a young girl to do.

Unsure of what else to do, Sarah reached out and shook Caitlin's hand, allowing her to get a close look at the little girl for the first time. Her freckled face was likely what everyone focused on when they were introduced to her. All Sarah could see were the bruises. As a child, Sarah had learned to wear long sleeves and grow out her hair for more effective concealment and she could see that Caitlin was making progress in this skillset but hadn't yet perfected it.

"My dad says that you're crazy."

Sarah considered the statement and the bluntness of children. Caitlin reminded her of a boy she once lived with, one of eight other children living in foster home number three. Luke had seen a lot of horrible things but he never lost his spirit and was always friendly to strangers when most of the other children would shrivel upon the threat of social interaction. The bespeckled girl before her had no business being so sweet and so talkative but she had held onto those qualities and Sarah was surprised at her own comfort with Caitlin's presence.

"Yeah? What do you think?" she asked the curious girl.

"I dunno. You seem nice to me," Caitlin made herself at home, sitting next to Sarah and dangling her feet over the edge of the platform. "My dad says a lot of things. I mean if you were crazy you'd be wearing a jacket, right?"

The bizarre statement confused Sarah. "What?"

"You know, a jacket with long sleeves that go like this," Caitlin wrapped her arms around her body and grabbed her shoulders.

Sarah smiled. "You're right. I guess that means I'm not crazy. It's good to know."

There had honestly been times when she wasn't so sure. It took a lot of crazy to grow up in the system and survive.

"You shouldn't smoke," Caitlin said bluntly. "It's bad for you."

With her eyebrows raised, Sarah turned to her new friend. Without breaking eye contact she flicked the cigarette over the edge and waited for Caitlin's approval.

"You shouldn't litter either."

Sarah laughed. The feeling struck her immediately as foreign. It had been years since she had laughed, at least in any way that was not meant to be sarcastic. Sarah looked at the little girl, appreciating her presence. She didn't know exactly how much they had in common but there was something there that bonded them and they both knew it. Sarah had tried so hard to remain in solitude her whole life, she wondered how many laughs she had missed.

Caitlin looked out over the alley and into the windows, Sarah was grateful that Miss Nipples wasn't putting on her show tonight. Caitlin's dirty blonde hair floated lightly in the wind, revealing a bruise that Sarah hadn't noticed before on her upper back.

"Do you love your daddy?" the words slipped out of Sarah's mouth. Unsure of why she even asked, she immediately regretted the decision.

"Yeah," the response was empty and rehearsed. Her eyes lowered to her swinging feet, she didn't like that Sarah wasn't giggling anymore.

Sarah's mind raced, she had done it now and there was no going back. If she was going to connect with this human, she felt that she needed to actually try. Making an effort to help or even know someone at all was something she had not done in a long time.

"Are you ever scared of your daddy?"

Caitlin lifted her legs and turned her body to Sarah, unwilling to meet her eyes.

"It's ok. It's ok to be scared sometimes," Sarah offered.

"I'm not scared," Caitlin shot back. The tone in her voice had changed and Sarah was no longer talking to a little girl. "My daddy loves me. He says I'm even prettier than my mommy."

The words felt like ice in Sarah's chest. Her mind raced at the thought of what they could mean and all of the worst possible options came to mind. Tears welled in her eyes but she held them back. Caitlin blinked and realized how she was speaking, she rested her posture and looked downstairs. The faint sounds of the argument had stopped.

"I got to go."

She stood and made her way down the stairs, her bare feet made almost no sound on the metal surface. Just before she reached the window Sarah called to her through the slats.

"If you ever need anything… I'm right upstairs."

Caitlin nodded and opened the window to the now quiet apartment. Sarah sat up straight and inhaled deeply, shocked at everything that just happened. Voluntary human interaction was not one of her normal habits and caring for strangers certainly wasn't either.

She lit another cigarette, even though she knew it was bad for her.

———

"I'm sorry, ma'am, unfortunately these muggings gone wrong are very common in the city. We are doing everything we can."

"I'm sorry, ma'am, there was no weapon found at the scene. No cameras nearby. I'm afraid there's just nothing we have to go on at this time."

"Listen, I'm sorry. I know. But you need to stop calling, it's only been a few days. We are doing everything we can."

It was the same every time. She had the homicide detective's number at the top of her favorites list since the day she met him and he had lost his sympathy for her it seemed. Kelli Armstrong had not stopped to mourn the death of her husband, she knew that was unhealthy but there was no space in her heart for self pity. Not yet.

She had run away and the memory of it haunted her. Looking back, that monster had put his knife into her husband's belly twice and she couldn't have stopped it, she knew that. She knew that if she hadn't run she would be dead too and Preston wouldn't have wanted that. But she had run to save herself and the thought of it was nearly enough to make her wish she had been lying in that alley with him.

Preston and Kelli married young, too young by the standards of just about everyone in their lives. Five years later they had learned a thing or two and began to see the magic fade a bit, which they privately admitted to themselves but never to each other. But the love was there. They still had that fairy tale romance and had turned their backs on the world so they could be together, passion was never their problem.

Kelli admitted to herself that her life had become entirely dedicated to Preston, leaving little room for friendships. Having gone down that path meant that she now had minimal support in her fight against the seemingly sluggish nature of the murder investigation but it also meant that she was more alone than she had ever been before. The quiet in the house was deafening. There were so many moments in every day that she knew she was supposed to see or hear Preston but then there was nothing. That, she thought, is what hurt the most; not necessarily his murder but his shocking absence. And she feared that feeling would never fade.

As she finished up her third phone call to the homicide detective that day, Kelli got into her car and started the engine. She knew before she pulled out of her driveway that there was nowhere to go, she just needed to drive. As she made her way down the suburban roads just outside downtown her vision became blurry. She came to a stop in the middle of an intersection and stared straight ahead.

At that moment, she could see nothing. Nothing was ahead of her, nothing was behind her. The world disappeared all around her and with it all sense of purpose. There were no sounds, no feelings, there was no reason to take the next step. Outside the car, in the real world, angry drivers pressed on their horns and shouted out their windows.

Kelli was suddenly woken back to reality when her phone began to vibrate in her lap. Realizing where she was and what she was doing, she pulled to the side of the road allowing the frustrated drivers to pass and take a look at the person who had inconvenienced them.

Safely tucked into the emergency lane, Kelli looked down at her phone. The display read "No Caller ID" and she considered ignoring it for a moment. Some government numbers don't allow callbacks, she thought to herself, it could be someone from the police. She answered the phone and a deep voice flowed from the speaker.

"Hello, Kelli."

———

Only a few hours had passed since the most shocking phone call of Kelli Armstrong's life. The urban legend known as The Good Samaritan was not only real but he had done what the police either couldn't or wouldn't do. When she first set eyes on him, she had it in her mind that she would hug him but quickly abandoned that plan. His presence was terrifying, she couldn't imagine what it must be like to be one of the criminals he brought to this horrible place.

Now she sat on a surprisingly comfortable couch in a room that was deeply unsettling despite several efforts to make it stand out from the rest of the warehouse. The Good Samaritan stood before her, he was dressed in a clean suit with no tie. His face glistened with sweat in the extreme heat of the old wooden building and she wondered why he insisted on dressing so formally.

He had just finished explaining to her that she was about to make a decision and that it would likely change her life. The murderer in the next room had admitted his guilt and had been subjected to so much pain that he was truly sorry for what he had done. The Good Samaritan explained that if this man were to go to prison, he would serve his time knowing that he was evil and that one day he would be released. It was time to decide whether he would live or die.

Kelli stood and with her hand on her belly took a deep breath, "I'm ready."

The two left the room and entered the main floor of the warehouse where Kelli could see the bloodied figure of a man tied to a chair. As she stepped into the light, her yellow sundress with a floral pattern shined brightly. She had done her hair as well, asking herself as she did it why she felt the need to be presentable for such an occasion. She confidently approached the man and felt that she commanded a certain respect thanks to her efforts.

Brett managed to lift his head just enough to see who had come to visit him, upon realizing it was the wife of his victim he began to weep. Kelli's eyes widened upon seeing the man's tears. She had cried more this week than she ever had, she had to make efforts to re-hydrate herself she had sobbed so deeply. And now this monster had the audacity to cry.

Kelli reached to the table of torture weapons and grabbed a knife. She lunged toward her husband's murderer and raised the knife over her head. As she thrust the knife towards Brett's neck, The Good Samaritan grabbed her wrist and stopped the blade from moving any further.

"I want this!" she screamed at him with fury.

The stranger simply shook his head silently.

"Fine," she stepped back and dropped the knife after he released her. "But I'm staying."

Typically it was standard to have the victims leave the room, the trauma of seeing someone murdered was great enough and The Good Samaritan usually insisted an innocent not endure it twice. But Kelli's mind was made up and he could see that. Without protest, he picked up the knife and stepped behind Brett.

Kelli breathed deeply as he lifted Brett's head by pulling on his brown hair. He held the knife to the killer's throat and looked up to once more confirm that this is what she wanted. In response, Kelli stepped closer to the men. The Good Samaritan slid the blade across Brett's throat, spilling blood down his chest and sending it spraying forward. The yellow flowers on Kelli's dress were ruined by drops of deep crimson. She never moved and she never looked away until the life had fully drained from Brett's body.

She turned to leave. "Wait," The Good Samaritan called after her.

She turned and he approached her, gesturing to her dress.

"That stays. To be burned."

She looked down and understood. "Okay. I have gym clothes in my car."

Kelli changed and handed the soiled dress to the man who had killed her husband's killer. She sighed as she passed the garment over, knowing that the dress had been worth more than the man's life and it was truly a shame that this evening came with a loss that actually meant something.

Chapter 21

The church was silent. John Corbin had only been in a catholic church a few times but every time he was impressed by the air of calm and quiet that they all seemed to maintain. It was simple to walk in and find someone to speak to, another foreign feeling as the churches he had always gone to were typically locked during the day on a weekday.

He sat in the pews, gazing up at the large crucifix mounted behind the altar. It had always been strange to him that the image of Christ dying was the chief representation of the catholic church. Jesus' sacrifice was of course an important part of his faith but he had never felt the need to worship his death. Crosses, too, held a similar stigma to him but not to the same degree. As he sat in such a peaceful and holy place he felt the need to pray but something about it felt vulnerable. Like he was taking off his shoes in someone else's house.

A priest entered the sanctuary and began going through some papers at a table near the side entrance, careful to be quiet so as to not disturb the detective. Corbin stood and approached the priest who introduced himself as Father Sherman. He was elderly but in good shape, sporting a white head of hair and a traditional black pants and shirt with a white collar.

The two spoke at length about the tragic death of Father Ellis who had been taken from this church before he met his demise. When Corbin asked about the day he was taken, Sherman admitted that he was not present that day but introduced the detective to a deacon named Armond, a younger man in his thirties. Armond had been preparing for the evening mass the day that Ellis had been taken and described the scene to Detective Corbin.

The deacon had been in the service of this church for many years and Corbin knew he had seen something, so he pushed further. After some conversation and maybe some mild intimidation he was able to convince Armond to reveal the truth about Father Ellis' vices behind closed doors.

Corbin thanked the man and left after he had been kind enough to reveal the name of the young lady who had been in the confessional that day; fifteen year old Lisa Harper.

———

The Harper residence was nestled in the quiet streets of Forest Hills, an upper class neighborhood and quite a long drive from the church. Corbin had heard of people driving further though, once you find a church that feels like home it is worth it. He rang the doorbell and it was promptly answered by Karen Harper who wore a warm smile.

"Yes?" Karen said curiously.

"Hello, ma'am. Detective John Corbin," he said as he held up his ID. "Is your daughter home?"

It was a concerning question for a detective to ask but Karen stepped back to reveal that her daughter was reading a book on the floor of the living room. A few moments later the three were all seated in the family room, Corbin sipping a freshly poured cup of coffee and Lisa doing her best to avoid eye contact and staying focused on her book.

"We were so shocked to hear about Father Ellis," Karen offered without being asked. "I try to keep Lisa as safe as possible. It's very scary to live in a world where someone would do that to an innocent priest."

The word *innocent* caused him to raise his eyebrows. "Oh, I know that the news said that he had done something wrong," she responded, not willing to share the details of the accusations in front of her innocent daughter. "But...well, if you knew Father Ellis, you would know that's a filthy lie." Lisa couldn't resist glancing up at her mother, seemingly offended by her naiveté.

"What was your relationship with Father Ellis?" Corbin asked after a sip of coffee.

"Well, nothing more than usual, I suppose. I mean he led the youth group, so we probably knew him a little better than the other clergy but we weren't particularly close."

"Where were you that day? The day he went missing." Corbin asked, noting that Lisa still had yet to look directly at him.

Karen was surprised by the question. "Why?"

"We just need to know every detail about the case. We've asked every member of the church the same question." It was a small lie but, he felt, an innocent one.

"Oh, well, I was at work and Lisa was at school."

Corbin looked again at the young Lisa Harper. They hadn't yet spoken to each other but the connection between them was significant. They were the only two people in the room who knew what this conversation was really about and Corbin could feel the tension permeate through the air. As he continued to speak he began ignoring Karen, focusing his attention on Lisa.

"I went to the church this morning. Talked to the clergy. They were the only ones around when it happened. They said they saw a tall man dressed in a suit remove Father Ellis from the confessional."

He set his coffee cup on the side table next to him and folded his hands.

"I asked the deacon, a man named Armond, who was in the confessional. He said he didn't know. So I asked again," he said, remembering that he had to raise his voice at the deacon and had pushed aside the guilt until later.

"He said that Father Ellis had been having inappropriate relations with a member of the youth." Karen became increasingly uncomfortable with the conversation. The man she invited into her home was not only accusing her priest of terrible things but he had become fixated on her daughter.

"He said that this girl had been coming to confess to him for three years now, and they always wound up in his office. He used to hear the girl's cries from the other side of the door." Armond's shame had been clear once he finally revealed the truth about the priest.

"Oh, my God," Karen finally interjected.

"I asked him who the girl was. He said her name was Lisa."

Karen's head snapped to her daughter. Her lip quivered and she begged with her eyes for Lisa to say something. "Lisa? Lisa, why would the deacon say that?"

"Where were you that day, Lisa?" Corbin pressed.

Karen's eyes filled with tears. Lisa closed her book and took several short breaths before turning to look Corbin in the eye.

"He got what he deserved," she said with a coldness that sent Karen into shock.

Corbin had gotten what he came for and stood without any expression on his face. He had never arrested a female teenager before and hoped that she would come willingly.

————————

The body of Brett McKinely had been delivered to those who had failed Kelli Armstrong. The Good Samaritan returned to the warehouse to continue disposing of the necessary evidence and disinfect the facility. As he passed through the main entrance he noticed Sarah hiding in the shadows and chose to ignore her presence, locking the door behind him and leaving her alone with her thoughts.

Inside, the clothes of both Brett and his victim's widow were tossed into the furnace. The tools were boiled in a large pot resting on a gas stove. The blood stained floor was sprayed with pressurized sodium hydroxide, a reasonably effective means of destroying DNA evidence although nothing is really fool proof, he had to admit. In the beginning, he had his choices of how he would be protecting himself and cleaning up after purifying twisted souls, bleach was on the list but he was uncomfortable with the idea of losing the lasting impression blood makes on a wooden floor. The sodium hydroxide was the best option but he was certain that if it ever became an issue, the deeper layers of wooden fibers would be irreversibly tainted. Were an investigative team ever to find this space, he simply hoped that the incredibly high volume of DNA samples found within the hardwood floor would be impossible to tell apart.

Satisfied with his work, The Good Samaritan decided to head home and spend time with Lily who had been seemingly frustrated with his absence as of late. This time Sarah did not hesitate to approach him as he locked the front door from the outside. He turned to head to his car but she blocked him, there was silence for a moment as he decided whether he needed to use violence to get rid of her. Her face was worn, it was clear that she had been crying.

"There's a little girl," she said with desperation in her voice. "She lives in the apartment below me. She... her father is... it's just like me."

She looked away, hoping that he would find some sympathy like he once did.

"Just like him," she whispered to herself.

He stepped around her without speaking and she followed him closely. "I-I'm not... doing good. I need you. I just... I fall apart when I don't see you. I don't know why. I need your help."

He reached the car and unlocked the door. Sarah didn't give up, "No... she needs your help."

"I already did your favor. I took care of the shop, that's all you get."

He slid into his vehicle and slammed the door. Sarah was taken aback by what she just heard. She rushed to the window and palmed the glass.

"What do you mean? The shop on MLK? You took care of that?"

He starts the car.

"But he's dead."

The engine cut off and The Good Samaritan stared straight ahead for a moment before turning to finally look her in the eyes.

"Those guys, they killed him yesterday," she said just loud enough to be heard through the glass. She had heard the news passing by a group of neighbors and listened in just long enough to learn that the old man had been murdered the night before. She hadn't been terribly surprised to learn it had happened but was heart broken to know that this man she looked up to had allowed it. Her faith in him had been momentarily shaken.

Suddenly he opened the door so quickly it nearly knocked her over. His towering mass rushed toward her and she instinctively walked backwards until the back of her head slammed into a telephone pole. As she recovered from the impact, he made a point to tower over her.

"But you did? You did go? They came back, why didn't you kill them? I told you what would happen. Why didn't you... ?"

He turned and returned to his vehicle. Sarah caught her breath and watched as the black sedan screamed through the gravel drive. She had never seen him so emotional and knew that the blood of evil men would be spilled that night.

———————

A cold blue light flickered across the living room from the TV, lighting the space in fleeting moments of digital luminance. Anthony wasn't really watching, but had to keep himself busy. He and Jose had been quarantining themselves in their apartments since the day before, just in case someone had seen them and they needed to stay off the streets. Anthony's mother had been begging him to run errands and he had to speak harshly with her to get her to stop.

The guilt over speaking to his mother that way was a heavier burden than yesterday's murder had been. This hadn't been his first killing and he was sure it wouldn't be his last. Sometimes things just had to be done, especially when his cash supply started hiring creepy enforcers to do their dirty work. If he had a choice the old man would have lived, but there wasn't any other way.

Suddenly the door swung open with a crack as the locks splintered off the door frame. For a fraction of a second, Anthony was able to see a dark figure enter the home and slam the door behind him.

"Mother fucker!" he shouted as he stood to tackle the home invader. The Good Samaritan easily dodged his attack and swiftly knocked him out cold with one punch to the jaw.

Anthony slowly awoke in a fog, not knowing for sure how much time had passed. He couldn't see past his knees but was able to tell that he was sitting in a chair. No, he was *tied* to a chair. Anthony struggled for a moment but was quickly able to see that he couldn't move at all. He tried to recall what had happened and how he got to be where he was. The vision of the tall stranger entering his home flashed in his mind.

He tried again to survey his surroundings as his vision slowly returned. The television was still the only light source in the room, he could see it about fifteen feet away along the left wall. But something created a shadow between Anthony and the light, he squinted again to see more clearly.

It was his mother. She too was tied to a chair from their dining room set, still dressed in her night gown. Her mouth was taped but her eyes were open and they begged her son for help that he could not offer.

"Ma?! Ma!" he cried out in desperation. "Help!"

Tears began to stream down his face just as The Good Samaritan appeared from the darkness and wrapped a roll of duct tape all the way around his head, not bothering to tear the strip but instead choosing to let the roll dangle at Anthony's shoulders. Panic set in and the young criminal furiously tried to negotiate with the ropes to no avail.

Anthony stopped struggling to take a closer look at his mother and apologize with his eyes. Whatever was about to happen was his fault, he knew that. Everything he had ever done was for her, now she was in danger and he was responsible for bringing this psychopath into their lives. He stared into her eyes wishing he could tell her everything and beg her forgiveness. That was when he noticed that his mother was dripping wet.

Confused, he looked closely and confirmed that every inch of her was soaked with a clear liquid. Around her, all of the living room furniture had been crudely pushed aside leaving her dead center. The floor had been coated with a thick layer of some sort of white spray that looked like styrofoam, the ceiling above her had been sprayed as well.

The terrifying situation had now taken on a bizarre tone which almost calmed Anthony, distracting him from his predicament, as he looked to the intruder for an explanation. The Good Samaritan slowly walked over to the woman and stood beside her, patiently reaching into his pocket and pulling out a box of matches. Anthony understood before the flame was lit and began to scream as much as he could behind his gag. The match slid along the powdered glass outside the box and sparked a small flame which he dropped into the old woman's lap.

The Good Samaritan stepped to the side as she immediately became engulfed in flames. Her painful screams could be heard through the tape and quickly weakened. Anthony struggled so much that his chair fell to its side. After slamming to the ground, his head faced the flames, forcing him to watch the agonizing death of the person he cared about most.

Once she stopped screaming, The Good Samaritan knelt down and lifted Anthony's head. The towering killer's face was black, the light from the fire behind him was so great. As he spoke to Anthony, the growling sound that came from his mouth sounded otherworldly and ushered in a sense of fear Anothony had never thought possible.

"Where's your friend?!"

———————

Cooking was never one of John Corbin's strong suits although he did pick up a few specialties in college thanks to a severe shortage of fresh ingredients in the dorm room. Jean and Bella, however, did not seem to appreciate the bachelor's cuisine he had offered at first and so he had to adapt. The newly full time single father was now dashing around the kitchen as he made his third attempt at spaghetti and meatballs but this time the meatballs were fresh and not from a frozen bag.

Jackson had been making a habit of visiting Corbin at home lately and sat on the kitchen counter sipping beer as he watched his partner look like a real person for a change. The visits had been awkward at first but the girls quickly took a liking to the young detective; Corbin theorized that this was because they had similar maturity levels.

"So what are you gonna do about the girl?" Jackson asked before taking a sip.

"What girl?"

"The girl. The priest killer."

Corbin tasted the sauce that was boiling on the stove. This was not like his mother's recipe. She probably didn't use the stuff from the can, he thought.

"Oh. Shit, I don't know. I don't have anything to charge her with really, until we catch him."

"Jesus Christ, do you realize how many people are going to jail when we catch this guy?" Jackson hopped off the counter and paced around the kitchen as they spoke. "They're gonna need their own prison. I've never seen so many accessories."

Corbin felt his phone ringing in his pocket and grabbed Jackson's free hand as he answered it, puppeting his partner's arm to continue tending to the meatballs that were almost done.

"Hello?" Corbin answered.

A gruff voice came from the other end of the line, *"John Corbin?"*

"Yeah."

"Yeah, hi, this is Detective Chuck Lambert, uh, I'm homicide over at the 14th. Listen, I got a crime scene over here...." Corbin had moved to his living room and was looking out the window as he listened. Lambert was struggling to say his next sentence as if the words were too ugly to say out loud.

"Well, I heard you were the guy checking out all the weird torture stuff, right?"

"Yeah, I guess." Corbin rolled his eyes, not sure if he was excited about that reputation.

"Well, if you like torture stuff, then you're gonna love this."

Corbin walked back into the kitchen and took the helm back from Jackson.

"Go across the hall and knock on the door. Ask for Mrs. Livingston," he ordered Jackson who seemed to understand without any further information. Corbin returned to the phone, "Ok Lambert, give me the details and we'll swing by."

———————

Detectives Jackson and Corbin pulled their vehicle up to the curb and got out to look up at a large apartment building effectively serving as a slum, just two blocks away from the Lucky Saver. The apartments all faced exterior hallways and could be clearly seen from the street. Corbin's attention was immediately drawn to the seventh floor where one doorway was garnished by black soot radiating from the door frame. A large collection of police officers, firefighters and onlookers pushed past each other in the narrow corridor.

The elevators were not functioning so the detectives began the long journey to the top of the steps where they pushed their way past the crowd and into apartment 7C. Chuck Lambert shook Corbin's right hand as he wiped the sweat from his forehead with the left.

"Hell of a month for the lift to break, huh?" Lambert spoke with a gruff voice. He was American through and through but every once in a while his British step-father's speech snuck out which always caught the attention of those around him. Detective Lambert was a large man, not terribly obese but far past his days of chasing down suspects on foot. His deep voice, red hair and thick mustache left an impression, Corbin was fairly certain they had met before.

"John Corbin," the exhausted detective said before pointing to his partner. "My partner, Jackson."

Lambert shook Jackson's hand as well and the three newly acquainted men stepped into the living room where a ghastly scene awaited them. Jackson hesitated before getting closer, first noticing the unmistakable smell of burnt flesh. Dead bodies were never pleasant but the unbearable scent seemed to permeate through every pore in his body.

After finding the courage to enter the room, Jackson studied the grim scene as best he could before closing his eyes. The room was centered around a body that had been burnt beyond recognition and bound to a metal chair. There were severe burn marks on the floor in a circle immediately surrounding the chair and heavy soot on the ceiling above. To his surprise, aside from the immediate area around the chair there was absolutely no burn damage at all. Rather, almost every surface within ten feet of the center of the room had been sprayed with some sort of white chemical.

About fifteen feet away from the body was a second corpse, also tied to a chair. The young man had what appeared to be several dozen stab wounds on his legs and a slice across his throat which Jackson assumed was the killing blow. His chair had fallen to the side and was resting in blood that had flooded the entire kitchen area.

The young detective turned to his partner. Corbin surveyed the scene with a coldness in his eyes. Jackson knew that enough years on the force could numb the shock of violent crime but this was something different entirely. Never having seen this type of carnage, Jackson found himself having a hard time even imagining a human being that was capable of this sort of rage.

"The kid, Anthony Burman." Lambert spoke up. "Small time crook, spends an average of one week in jail every month. The Cajun corpse? That's his mother as far as we can tell. This is her place and her estimated height matches the neighbor's descriptions."

Corbin stepped in for a closer look at the mother as Lambert continued, "M.E. Says that the stab wounds in the kid's leg are the cause of death. Bled right out. The necklace there was just to be sure, almost no blood after that cut."

Jackson decided to examine the wounds on Anthony's legs, comforting himself with the familiar environment of puncture wounds.

"Whoever set dear mum here on fire, used some sort of flame retardant to contain the flames. Fire stayed in the middle of the room and never spread."

"Oh shit," Jackson uttered from the kitchen.

"What?" Corbin joined his partner. Jackson was holding his phone in his hand which displayed one of the photographs he had taken of Father Ellis' body, zoomed in on his leg wounds. He held the phone near Anthony's leg to compare the two.

"It's him," Jackson proclaimed.

"No, that doesn't make sense," Corbin was quick to respond. "None of this is right. Why would he do it here? It's too sloppy, too last minute. And the mom doesn't make sense, why would he kill the mom?"

Corbin mentally flipped through dozens of evidence folders searching for similarities. Everything about this scene went against his understanding of who this killer was. As much as he was a genuine sociopath, if there was anything to respect about the man it was his precision. Absolutely nothing about this crime had been planned aside from the chemical fire retardant and he had never heard of a single victim being killed within a time frame of any less than five days.

He couldn't shake the feeling though, something about it was familiar. There was a passion to the work that was difficult to describe. So many murders are about the death itself, these killings were always about the process. It was never that they died but rather how they died.

"Man, it's just his style, though." Corbin was not speaking to anyone in particular. "I get why he'd do the kid, but everybody we've ever gotten has been guilty. Why the mom?"

"I mean what's this kid into?" Jackson offered. "Do we know whether the mom was a part of it? Something like that?"

Corbin's chest turned frigid. He couldn't imagine a more terrible way to die than watching your own mother burn to death as you bled out on your kitchen floor. Jackson was almost relieved to see the disturbed look on his partner's face to confirm that he did indeed have a soul.

"What?"

"Killing the innocent for a more effective torture," Corbin spoke quietly. "He's slipping. He's never done this before. It's always planned, always careful, always rational." He turned to Lambert, "Where did you say the other body is?"

"Two floors up. Same thing with the legs," Lambert responded.

"What was the time of death on that one?" Corbin began to visualize the gruesome process of committing three murders in less than an hour.

"Not long ago. Like thirty minutes."

The senior detective's mind raced. This sort of active perspective on these killings was a completely different investigation. They were always one day, ten steps behind this man. The game was always played on his court with his sadistic rules that changed daily. Killing people in their home seemingly on a whim was sloppy and criminals who made mistakes like that could be caught.

"Let's go. Thanks, Lambert." Corbin ushered Jackson away from the crime scene and they began the long descent down to ground level. There was no time to waste, Corbin thought, if there was ever a time that this master of murderous precision could be caught then this was it. The evening heat made the descent all the more arduous but Corbin couldn't resist the temptation of imagining what it would be like to apprehend his prey. The years of chasing him had been long and they very likely may have cost him his marriage. John Corbin proudly considered himself to be a pessimist in most circumstances, he felt it made him good at his job, so glimmers of hope were foreign and uncomfortable.

Just across the street a stranger observed the scene from the shadows. The Good Samaritan found a perch of darkness in a small park with very little green. Many years ago the city had run an obligatory campaign of installing small parks no bigger than nine hundred square feet all across the city in an effort to seem more "green." The effort had gone mostly uncelebrated but made for enough good headlines to be considered a mission accomplished.

Corbin approached his vehicle and from a distance The Good Samaritan set eyes on the man who was chasing him for the first time. He had been tempted in the past to find a way to see the detective in person so that he could better read his quality but the risk never outweighed the potential benefits. Sarah had made it quite clear how dangerous it could be to do something as reckless as attempt to hide yourself among a crowd when observing this man.

The Good Samaritan had to admit that what had transpired that night was the product of an emotional reaction and far outside the guidelines he had made for himself many years earlier. He felt that it was time to learn more about the man who would be piecing together clues that could have been left in the careless act.

Detective John Corbin carried himself like a man who kept his body in shape without letting such pursuits take over his life. His eyes were sad and his gate was confident, an intriguing mix that suggested a pride in his work and anxiety elsewhere. His clothes were sized properly but not tailored, therefore his shirt was slightly too baggy in the torso, likely a choice made by either a lack of interest in mens fashion, lack of funds or both.

The detective got into his vehicle and started the engine. The young man he was with followed shortly after and the two began to pull out of the parking lot. Suddenly a strange sense of reckless abandon overcame The Good Samaritan and he stepped ever so slightly into the light.

As Corbin neared the exit of the parking lot he caught a glimpse of a stranger in the shadows across the street. The face was unmistakable. He had seen so many artist portrayals, he had heard so many eye witness testimonies, the man had been in so many of his nightmares. Now, just forty feet away a cold face stared back at him.

Time slowed to a crawl. Corbin finally witnessed for himself the chilling blue eyes that seemed to glow in the darkness, the slender face and strong jaw that was the last thing so many people saw before they died. And a suit, of course he was wearing a damn black suit in the hottest summer on record. The man that the papers called The Good Samaritan looked deep into Corbin's eyes as the seconds passed by like minutes.

Suddenly the stranger broke his gaze and turned to a vehicle on a collision course with the detective's car. Corbin had pulled too far into the road.

"John!" shouted Jackson as the oncoming car blared its horn and attempted to stop. The vehicles collided, sending Corbin's car spinning back into the parking lot. Shattered glass seemed to levitate all around them as the sound of squealing tires and crunching metal filled the warm air. Corbin's head slammed into the driver's side window as they slid to a halt, cracking the glass and opening a fresh cut on his temple.

The dazed detective stumbled out of his vehicle as a small group of officers ran to the scene and began frantically checking on his well being. He waved them off and looked back across the street in search of the enigma that had distracted him. Nothing.

An angry and battered driver began shouting obscenities at Corbin, words that he could barely hear due to what was likely a concussion. If he was concussed it wouldn't be for the first time but he had been a young man when it happened last. Corbin continued to scan the area for the stranger, beginning to doubt his own eyes. Had it been real? He had seen the psychopath many times in his sleep but never full blown hallucinations. This man was a surgeon when it came to murder, he wouldn't seriously be stupid enough to stick around and take in the sights after committing possibly his most terrible crime yet.

Corbin considered telling Jackson to send out a search but reminded himself that teams were already out there. The man was an expert at remaining in the shadows and had managed to remain nearly undetected across the street from a dozen police officers. The clock was ticking on his investigation and there wasn't much time left until the chief pulled the plug. Now, more than ever, there was a chance to end this.

Chapter 22

The Child Services administrative building was located just east of downtown which seemed like an effort to make sure it was within a short distance from other government buildings but an intentional statement that it was non-essential. In the city, improvements were driven by political advancements. The last few mayors all had their platforms that they could now claim as their crowning achievements during their tenures but the new recycling program and tourism dollar generating pier could do little to help children in need.

Detective John Corbin pushed through the main entrance and studied the minimalistic seventies era interior design that was clean but badly in need of an update. To his right a handful of chairs were arranged in an open square and were half filled with people who didn't want to be there. That must be the case just about every time, Corbin thought.

Cobin headed to the front desk with a determined pace. Things were headed in the right direction and he was determined to make absolutely certain that nothing impeded the forward progress. He placed his badge on the desk as he approached.

"Detective Corbin, twenty third precinct," he said bluntly. "I need to see a case file and to speak with the counselor representing that case."

The front office administrator was a seasoned veteran of the Child Services department. Kristen Morgan was approaching her twenty fifth year of interacting with the very worst kinds of people and caring for the most innocent. She had long ago become defensive of not only the children but anyone who dared to disrespect her or the mission of this place. She had a very short fuse for men in particular and approaching her without so much as a smile or a good morning and then expecting her to jump for him was not well received.

"You can't just come in here," Kristen started. "That's confidential and you would need a warr-"

Before she could finish her sentence, Corbin had revealed a folded slip of paper from his inside jacket pocket. A few minutes later, Detective Corbin was being escorted down the well lit carpeted hallways. The warrant had been surprisingly easy to get. He knew it would get approved but the speed with which the judge signed it surprised him. Corbin reminded himself that things were finally headed in the right direction and that he could allow himself to expect good fortune now and then.

Corbin was introduced to Ashley Boone, a social worker with the Child Services department who seemed too young to have treated Sarah Thomson. Her brown hair rested just above her shoulders but would have been much longer if not for the curls. She wore a blue pantsuit and comfortable looking flats. Her face was beautiful but understated, a quality Corbin would be looking for if he were considering entering the dating pool at all.

"She was deeply disturbed when she arrived," Ashley Continued. "Her time here was helpful but unfortunately cases like hers rarely have happy endings."

Corbin was trying to keep up with the woman who was clearly in a hurry to be somewhere, he was holding a manilla folder she had given him and trying to search through its contents without tripping. He lifted a small photograph of Sarah at what looked to be about the age of fourteen. Though not exactly a professional photo, Corbin could see a great sadness in her eyes. She seemed alone.

"I know she's been in a lot of trouble, but trust me, she wouldn't even be alive if she hadn't come here. She'd been through a lot in her life."

Corbin nodded and continued to search the paperwork, "Her father was killed, do you know anything about that?"

"In a way. His murder was obviously the reason she was sent in for treatment. So I know what you know for the most part. She didn't like to talk about it. She had a nervous tick, she would rub her hands together, the only time she stopped was when we tried to get her to talk about her father's disappearance. While she refused to discuss it, the topic almost seemed to soothe her, which is obviously bizarre."

Corbin scanned through notes taken during Sarah's sessions as they rounded a corner, "You think he abused her?"

"Unquestionably. She has permanent scars, you can't hide that kind of abuse. She had a physical exam upon admittance. Doctors said that she wouldn't be able to carry children."

He met her eyes to acknowledge that he understood what she was saying. The girl had certainly been through an unimaginable pain, he reminded himself that knowing this didn't change the facts of the case. A moment later he remembered having provoked her with memories of her past back at the precinct and a wave of guilt rushed over him.

They stopped in front of a door that was closed, "Look. I never met the father, obviously. And I don't make a lot of statements like this. But we see a lot here, we try to heal a lot of scars that we know have no hope of ever healing. A lot of people do a lot of terrible things to innocent people and just walk away. This guy, whatever happened, he got what he deserved. I'm sorry detective, I'm already late."

"No, of course. Thank you for your time."

"Good luck," she said as she opened the door and walked through. Inside, Corbin caught a glimpse of a young boy waiting for his therapy session. In the brief moment he looked like an ordinary child but Corbin found himself wondering what terrible truths lay beneath the surface.

As the detective left the building he contemplated this world he spent his life protecting and wondered how much of it was really worth saving.

———————

Lily awoke from a quiet sleep and reached for her glass of water on the bedside table. Finding it empty, she slid out of bed and left the bedroom with a drowsy gate. Her nightgown shimmered in the moonlight as she passed the row of hallway windows. Their home was so big, she often thought, it would be nice if one day it was filled with little ones to make it seem smaller. But she knew that had never been an option.

She carefully descended the steps, straining her eyes to see in the darkness. She had always been comfortable at night, appreciating the beauty of the slivers of light that guide the way. There was a simple kind of magic in walking in near blindness with only small clues and muscle memory to aid you.

As she approached the kitchen her thoughts once again turned to the family she would never have. Her husband was an honorable, intelligent and wealthy man (not to mention incredibly handsome with eyes that nearly hypnotized you). But he had told her early on that he learned at a young age he was sterile. She knew he wasn't the type of man you let slip away so she set aside any dreams of children she once had so that the two of them could build a life together.

Very little about their marriage was what she had imagined as a little girl, but life was good and comfortable. Although he was working most of the time, when she was in his presence it felt like no harm could ever come to her. When he looked into her eyes all it ever took was just the slightest smile and she would feel a warmth flow through her that washed away the loneliness she felt when he was gone.

She pulled a water glass from the cupboard and began to fill it. Yes, she thought, everything is good. With very little exception, this life of hers was better than anything she could have dreamt as a child. She turned to go back to bed and saw a dark figure in the corner of her eye. Frightened, she shouted and dropped the glass on the tile floor sending glass and water in every direction around her feet.

Lily looked again at the figure in the shadows, it was her husband. "Jesus, you scared me."

The Good Samaritan turned to look at her, his bright blue eyes shining through the darkness in a way that almost seemed supernatural. He sat at the end of the dining room table holding a glass of bourbon in his hand. Lily always made sure to keep his favorite brand in supply although she had never actually seen him drink it.

"I didn't even know you were back, why didn't you call me? How was your trip?" she said as she carefully tiptoed around the glass and into the dining room which was free of any dangers.

"It was fine," he responded dismissively.

She kissed him on the cheek and sat down next to her husband. The clock on the wall seemed to tick louder than ever as she wondered what that response meant and why he had returned ahead of schedule. Staying on schedule was very important to him and she knew to always expect an unwavering obedience to their calendar.

"I've missed you, I've been so bored without you," she said with a small chuckle, trying to break the silence. It wasn't entirely true. She had her girlfriends in town and ran an Etsy shop that was doing very well these days. She always found ways to keep herself busy but she did miss him when he was gone.

The Good Samaritan stared at his drink, not interested in the light banter Lily was trying to engage in. The amber liquid slid effortlessly around the crystal as he rotated the glass in his hand. He had rarely chosen to partake in drinking alcohol but appreciated its craftsmanship. In an effort to maintain his image as a typical husband he would slowly empty the bottle in the liquor cabinet down the drain over a few weeks, regretting that doing so was a waste.

The slow conversation was not unusual, Lily was used to nearly complete silence from her husband, but something was different. "What is it, what's the matter? Is anything wrong at work?"

He shook his head no and allowed himself a small sip of the liquor. Doubt crept into Lily's mind, wondering what the problem could possibly be if not a work issue. Why would he come home early if everything was going well at work? Was it something she had done? Or not done?

She forced a smile hoping it would outshine her worried eyes, "Is everything ok with me?"

He closed his eyes, realizing he had allowed the mistakes he had made this week to seep into other areas of his life and behaving this way was risking too much. He lifted his head and looked deep into her eyes with a smile that was genuinely sympathetic but did not show his teeth. He took her hand and held it in his, the size difference was almost comical.

"I love you," said Lily with a sigh of relief.

He squeezed her hand without responding and stood. He then stepped onto the sodden kitchen floor and began to pick up the pieces of glass one by one. Lily admired her husband as he did so, grateful to have him home. The Good Samaritan looked over to his wife and saw that she was bleeding from her right heel and hadn't yet noticed.

He stood and wet a white kitchen towel at the sink. Kneeling before her, he lifted her foot and pressed it lightly against the wound. Only at this moment did Lily realize she had been cut and suddenly felt the pain. Her husband carefully patted the area and allowed the blood to soak into the towel. She ran her fingers through his blonde hair, appreciating the protector that she had married.

After a few moments the blood clotted and he was able to remove the towel without further bleeding. He poured her another glass of water and led her back upstairs where he tucked her into bed and watched her drift to sleep.

Lily was more important to him than she would ever know. If she ever did learn the truth she would likely kill him herself.

Chapter 23

The city was host to no less than forty five privately owned coffee shops. The cheapest and by far the easiest to get to from the precinct was on the same block and proudly boasted a large sign that read "Coffee Shop" in bold blue letters. Never quite sure if it had a different name, officers had long referred to it as simply "The Coffee Shop" and it was the go-to caffeine source for the twenty third.

For years they had offered a simple menu; drip coffee that was most often served black. As the market changed the shop owners began to feel the pressure of a changing industry and invested in what appeared to be a Keurig on steroids which could produce a TV-Dinner-esque version of a latte. Occasionally, a member of Gen-Z would stumble in hoping that the exterior was an ironic facade hiding a modern coffee house filled with world class baristas and it was only during these times was the machine even turned on.

Detective John Corbin sat at one of four small round tables made of aluminum inside the cramped coffee shop. On the table were several small stacks of papers, two porcelain coffee cups and the sweaty hands of one Warren Sheffield. The former pupil of The Good Samaritan had been rambling on for some time and Corbin was beginning to notice he had only really heard a small portion of what he was saying. This meeting was Warren's idea and he had insisted it happen this day.

"Ok so next thing," continued Warren, "I'm thinking, is the flyers. I had these made at the copy place last night, check this out."

He proudly slid the top copy out of a brown paper bag to present a crudely enhanced version of the artist sketch of The Good Samaritan that Simon had produced. The man was already menacing enough but Warren had altered the lines to be thicker and darker, successfully producing a more vicious aesthetic. The flier also offered the precinct's phone number and a brief description of The Good Samaritan's crimes.

"Try and hide now, you bastard. Huh?" Warren grunted with a smile.

He rested the paper on top of the bag it came from and began to pull out a variety of other publications. "And that's just the beginning, I got a ton of stuff here. Like uh, this, this is a description of the warehouse. At least, what I saw. I figure maybe somebody was there before it was his, maybe someone will know."

Warren's tone was irritating to Corbin. This man had first approached him as a victim, a scared little roach hiding from its would-be killer. There was an odd humility to his initial pleas for help, a vulnerability that came with knowing he would likely meet a gruesome end as a punishment for talking. But that vengeance never came. Corbin had waited each day for the news that the killer had slipped past the protective detail. It was clear at this point that The Good Samaritan had no intention of putting this man down as long as he stayed within the law.

But now that his relative safety had reassured Warren the humility was all but gone. He had doubled his efforts lately and had been requesting more time with the homicide detective. Corbin watched as the once victim proudly wore the hunter's mask and wondered how much he had in common with this man. At what point was the pursuit of this evil an unhealthy obsession? When does one look the other way in favor of focusing on his own mental health?

The waitress walked past and Warren anxiously pointed to his cup, "Excuse me, miss?"

She refilled his cup and offered some to Corbin who waved her away without speaking. Warren studied the Detective's demeanor and knocked on the table.

"Hey, what's the deal? Are you listening to any of this?"

"Yeah, I got it, Warren."

"Well, what the hell then?"

Corbin sat back in his chair, still not looking at Warren or his hard work. He picked up his coffee and took a slow sip. He had always preferred a little cream but his co-workers all took it black and after some peer pressure he found that the cream completely destroyed the flavor. He took in the strong scent and considered his next words carefully.

He looked up at the disfigured man, "I need to ask you something. And whatever the answer is, it stays between us."

Warren sat back in his chair, relieved to hear the detective finally speak. He waved his hand and raised his eyebrows as if to say "well go ahead, then."

"What'd you do?"

Warren tilted his head in confusion. For any ordinary person it would be reasonable to wonder why they were asked this question at all but he already knew the answer to that. What intrigued him was very simply, why now? Warren assumed this would come up the first day but it never did.

"They've all done something," Corbin continued. "I got a pervert priest, an abusive father, a hit and run, and that's just this month. So, I'm just wondering; which one are you?"

Corbin almost felt disgusted with himself, reducing the list to such a small selection. He knew each and every case and could have gone on for an hour. Warren's lips curled into a grotesque partial smile as he admired the detective across the table. Corbin had made it clear he was a relatively non-confrontational person and Warren knew this question was well outside his comfort zone.

"Okay. Yeah, I was a bad guy. I was a bad father." Warren's voice was sincere as he dropped his smile and reflected on his own past. "I did a lot of things I shouldn't have, things I could never even talk about. I did them and they were awful. But I'm a different man now. I've changed. I'm sober. I love my son, I would never hurt him again. Ok? Does that answer your question? I'm not on your list of bad guys because I'm not that guy. Not anymore."

Child abuse. There were few things Corbin despised more in the world than grown men willing to raise a fist to a child. Even one who had supposedly found salvation.

Corbin pressed further, "Is that because of him? Did he do that?

"I guess. I'd like to think I would've changed on my own, but you know what? That's probably not true, so yeah, it's because of him." Warren paused for a moment, surprised to hear himself admit it. "Does that make what he did a good thing? That make him some kind of a hero? Who's side are you on, John?"

"I'm on the side of the law, Warren."

"Good. Can we get back to this now?"

"Yeah, go ahead."

The victim turned hunter spent the next twenty seven minutes going through his campaign to do his part to catch the killer. Corbin was grateful for the clock mounted on the wall behind Warren which allowed him to track the minutes until he had to leave.

Corbin gave Warren his blessing to do as he wished, now confident that he would be safe from retribution.

In all fairness, jovial feelings had been something of a rarity for Warren Sheffield ever since he had been purified. Every moment since that time had been a slowly diminishing anxiety overdrive. It had been fourteen months and twelve days since his son was escorted into the warehouse and played judge and jury over Warren's battered form.

The flood of confusion he had felt when Kyle forgave him had been mixed with a rush of guilt, relief and extreme fear of what would come next. It was months before he could even look his son in the eyes, terrified that he would make a mistake and be taken once again. But the months passed and his torturer stayed away, Warren would sometimes think that he caught glimpses of him in crowds and through a dark window but he was never sure.

Kyle, too, learned to warm up to his father. He knew that he had a certain power over him that most children do not have but it wasn't long before their newfound mutual respect blossomed into something that resembled a normal father and son relationship, or as much of one as either of them could expect. Kyle was always careful to avoid discussing his mother, whose departure had been the catalyst for his father's drinking habit, just in case it would trigger him back to the old ways.

For Warren, however, even the relative salvation of his relationship with his son could not erase the trauma of his experience with The Good Samaritan. The scars, both internal and external, would never heal and they plagued him constantly. He felt that he could have handled much of that and worked through it but it was the looks from passersby on the streets that kept him locked in a state of resentment. His face was truly a disturbing sight, not that he had been very handsome before the mutilation. The horrified stares from all who were unfortunate enough to catch a glimpse reminded Warren every day that he craved revenge.

As he walked home from work, he reflected on the past few weeks. A sense of control, power even, had overtaken him. Warren had faced his darkest fears in every way and was now chasing after them with murderous intent. He knew in his heart that he would catch The Good Samaritan and he'd be a hero for his efforts. This feeling of elation felt so foreign he wondered if he had ever felt it before.

The trip home always included pretending not to see several liquor stores and bars, ignoring them had gotten easier with time. Perhaps that truly exceptional feeling he had was why he was suddenly noticing them again. Before long the reason why didn't really matter but that first drink, sitting alone at what was once his favorite bar near the house, tasted like a hard earned reward. It was a familiar place to be, sitting there on that stool holding the cool glass in his hand. It felt like home.

When Warren fumbled his keys into the front door, hours after he was supposed to be home, Kyle's heart stopped. These were sounds he knew well and he hadn't heard them in well over a year. Kyle slid into his room and locked the door behind him.

Maybe they should have moved, Warren thought to himself as he entered the home, after his wife had left. It likely would have been better not to come home every day to the drapes that she picked out, the carpet she had insisted on instead of the tile that he wanted, the wall she had painted green which matched her eyes. They had been so happy, the two of them. Raising a family was always a dream of hers and even though Warren had never planned to be a father he was happy to build a family with her. Anything for the woman he loved.

Warren stumbled to his knees, tears in his eyes. Before him, a photograph had been resting face down for years. He had been afraid to look at it. Filled with confidence built on a foundation of beer and vodka, Warren lifted the frame and studied the two happy faces. A younger, much better looking Warren stood with his arms wrapped around the love of his life. His reason for being. The picture had been taken on her birthday, just one year before Kyle had been born. They were truly happy.

But something changed when he arrived. The light within her was shut out and everything that made her who she was vanished. The doctor's called it postpartum depression, Warren never took the time to learn what that actually meant. All he knew was that it was common for mothers and that it would pass. The change never went away. As her resentment for each of them grew, she became more and more distant.

When Kyle was just over two years old, Warren came home one day to find she had left without packing a single thing including their child who was alone in his room. That day, Warren looked at the photograph one last time before placing it face down on the shelf. His reason for being had left. She had been poisoned by a son that he had never wanted.

In his drunken state he wiped the years of dust off the frame and placed it upright where it belonged before struggling back up to his feet. Though Kyle's room was just twenty feet away, it took a surprisingly long time to walk there.

"Kyle! You in there?"

Behind the locked door, Kyle's heart raced. He had extensive experience with taking care of his father in severely inebriated states but this was different. This was one of the bad times. He jumped back at the sound of Warren's obese body slamming into the locked door.

"Kyle!" he grunted loudly from behind the wood. "You unlock this goddamn door right now!"

Another loud thud and more tears slid down Kyle's face. He looked around his room, mad at himself for ever being alone without a phone. He knew better. Suddenly, the door frame splintered and Warren's hulking body tumbled into the room, blocking the exit. Kyle stood up and approached his father in a feeble attempt to help.

"Dad, come on, let me help-"

Warren shoved Kyle back into the dresser, knocking the lamp onto the floor. The room was now filled mostly with shadow as Kyle watched the sloppy but massive form of his father tower over him and pull him up by his shirt.

"You know, your mother...never wanted you. She thought she did. But as soon as she laid eyes on you she hated you."

Kyle struggled to free himself from his father's thick fingers. Warren pulled him in close, exhaling saturated, alcohol infused breath.

"You were the reason we had fights, the reason we had no life, the reason she wasn't happy. And when she left, I was all alone. I loved her so much. And she left me here with you. Stuck with you."

With his eyes closed, Warren reached his fist back and struck his son with all his strength. His nose broken, Kyle was once again forced into the dresser. This time, Warren did not wait to see if his son would stand and dropped to his knees. He struck the boy once again with a closed fist across the right cheek. The physical effort exhausted him but he inhaled deeply through his sweaty lips and wondered to himself what if he were to hit him so hard that he killed him? Would she come back?

Warren pulled his arm back a third time and readied the attack. Just as he began to push his fist forward a powerful grip yanked him across the room, his head slamming against the opposite wall. It had been difficult to distinguish objects through his drunken haze as it was but the impact on his skull worsened the effect. Warren tried to make out the dark figure that now loomed overhead. It was him.

Kyle opened his eyes for long enough to see The Good Samaritan kneel beside his father and put a blade to his throat. His sharp blue eyes turned and asked Kyle for permission to dispatch the drunken coward. Kyle looked at his father one last time as he began to realize what was happening and made a pitiful effort to escape The Good Samaritan's grasp.

The young man pushed himself up to make sure he could see and nodded in agreement. The man shrouded in darkness quickly pulled the blade across Warren's throat and stood as the torrent of blood slid down his chest. The Good Samaritan stepped to the doorway and watched the pool of red spread across the floor and touch Kyle's bare feet. The boy didn't move and seemed comforted by the warmth of the wetness as the life drained from his father.

The Good Samaritan took one last look at Warren to see the light fade from his eyes then sheathed his blade and placed it in his inside jacket pocket before re-fastening the top button. Kyle never broke eye contact with his father as his protector turned and left his life.

Chapter 24

It had rained earlier in the evening which helped to cool the bricks in the alley behind Tap Seventeen. Sarah pushed her way out the back door and immediately lit a cigarette. The streetlamps reflecting off the shimmering bricks provided a soothing glow. These days she didn't get flustered by something as pathetic as a shift manager but she found her heart racing after the scene that had just taken place.

She had lost her temper, she supposed. That was nothing new for her. Of the long list of jobs she had held in her young life it would be accurate to say that a short fuse had led to most of them being terminated. She kept her cool for the most part this time, until her shift manager finally told her to leave at which point she shattered a handful of plates against a wall that she knew had been suffering from water damage. Sarah hadn't expected the roach infestation living within the wall but the chaos that followed the barrier being broken was a welcome bonus.

Shortly after stepping into the soggy alley, Casey the bartender caught up to her.

"Sarah, I am so sorry. He had no right to talk to you like that."

"It's fine," Sarah turned to him but didn't look up. "Really."

"No, I mean, you've been kind of off lately, but... damn. I mean do you have another job anywhere or...?"

It was sweet, his child-like charm. Sarah made an effort to be sure that no one would ever have any good reason to show her kindness but Casey was either too kind or too dumb to care.

"No, but it's ok. It'll be ok," she breathed in from her cigarette as she considered her own words. It was true, she somehow always seemed to make things work. Quite often it was just a few days before rent was due but she always managed to find a way.

"So, what are you gonna do now?"

"I don't know. I guess I'll figure something out."

She knew that was true, it had been for a long time. The job was forgettable, a flashing moment in the complex but not lengthy history that was her "career". Something had been wrong lately and she knew it at her core.

The continued failed attempts at being The Good Samaritan's lap dog had eaten away at her. She had been asking herself why she kept going back. Sarah thought she had done a good thing by helping him find the shop on MLK but he ignored her and the man died. Sarah was never big on empathy but some things are just wrong and the murdering of innocents falls neatly in that category. So why did he just let it happen?

She knew her obsession with the vigilante killer was not healthy, but something had always compelled her to keep going back. It wasn't exactly something she could discuss with a shrink so she had never really challenged herself to find meaning in it. One thing she knew was that enough time had passed that whatever it was she was searching for it was clear she wasn't going to get it. A wasted effort.

Sarah finally looked up at Casey. He really was quite handsome. Not in a way that most women would look for but there was an innocence to his face that she found endearing.

She whispered mostly to herself, "I just need to try something else."

Her cigarette dropped to the wet bricks as she stepped toward him and lifted herself up onto her toes, he was nearly a foot taller than her. She pulled him in close by his neck and kissed his lips. Shocked by the sudden intimate gesture, Casey was unsure of how to react but after a moment closed his eyes and pressed into the warmth of her lips. He pulled back just far enough to speak.

"Sarah...what are you...?"

"Isn't this what you wanted?" she whispered.

She kissed him again, this time pressing harder. Casey wrapped his arms around her waist and pulled her in tightly. The feeling of her body against his was as he had imagined it, a pleasant blend of warm, firm and soft. His blood rushed and he lifted her as she wrapped her legs around him. He swung her around and pushed her back against the alley wall as she pushed her tongue into his mouth.

"We need to go," he whispered through heavy breaths.

———————

Sarah waited for Casey to fall asleep before lighting her cigarette, he had said something about the building being non-smoking. She lay on her back with the street lights streaming through the window on her face, Casey passed out shortly after they had finished and turned to his side. It had been a year or so since she had been nude in anyone's sheets but her own and she found herself jealous of whatever thread count Casey had invested in.

She was no expert on sex but felt like the bartender held his own, he even went for two rounds. Orgasms were never a priority for her which was good because no man had ever given her one. Sarah had to admit that the warmth of his touch had been welcome and something she was almost embarrassed to feel the need for.

Sarah pulled the sheets down slightly to reveal Casey's back, a small scar could be seen just outside his spine on his low back. Curious to hear the story, she regretted for a moment that they would never see each other again so she could ask. The sex had been pleasant but in the end she knew that's all it was. Whatever it was that she was looking for she didn't find it in his arms or between his legs.

The cool tile was refreshing as she stood to gather her clothes, silently slipping them on as she walked barefoot to the door of the apartment. Before leaving she looked back at Casey. He was a good man, she knew that, and in a world where she deserved to live that life she might have even chosen to stay. But that was not where she would find meaning, he could never give her what she needed. Whatever elusive force that was.

Chapter 25

Detectives Corbin and Jackson pushed through the crowded narrow corridors of the twenty third precinct. Corbin had always felt like humans must have been much smaller when they originally designed most of the buildings in the city, getting from one place to another often felt like ants sliding through tunnels.

"Oh, and that reporter called," Jackson updated his partner. "Says she wants the inside story on The Good Samaritan."

Corbin turned to the young detective with a disappointed glare. "What?" Jackson defended. "If they're gonna call him that, we might as well too. Come up with your own name if you want."

Corbin decided to ignore the pedestrian use of words and pressed on.

"Anyway, I told her we can't talk to her and she knows that. That's what a P.I.O. is for. Jesus Christ, you'd think that'd be the first thing they teach you in reporter school. 'Leave the fuckin' cops alone, they couldn't help you even if they didn't think you were a half assed reporter', who needs a nose job by the way."

The two men finally reached their squad room. Upon entering Corbin immediately noticed a young boy sitting with a detective, it was Kyle Sheffield. His face had been treated for what looked like serious injuries.

"What is this? Why the hell is he here?" panic had gripped John Corbin.

Jackson felt helpless and embarrassed to be behind on what he knew was important information, "Shit. I don't know, man."

Corbin rushed towards Kyle but stopped dead in his tracks when he noticed Captain Morton standing in his office doorway. The look on his face was, for once, that of sincere sympathy. He gestured for the two men to join him.

A few moments later Captain Morton finished filling in the detectives on the gruesome crime scene that Kyle had waited a full twenty four hours to report. Corbin kept his emotions contained, waiting for the punchline. It couldn't be true, he thought. After everything that had happened, this couldn't be the end. He was so close.

"Fuck! God damn it! What the-? Where was the protective detail?"

"They were there, they didn't see anything," the Captain defended. It was true, the small team of two police officers had not left their post all night.

"Probably asleep, who'd they put out there?"

"It doesn't matter."

"Fuck!" Corbin picked up a folder of papers from the Captain's desk and tossed it at the window in a rageful moment he immediately recognized as childish. The shouting had already attracted the attention of most of the squad room who were now watching them like it was a fish tank.

"Hey, hey, hey! Don't throw my shit around!" Morton pushed him back. "Look, John I'm sorry, you can't do this anymore."

With that statement, John Corbin's eyes widened and he stared his Captain down.

"It was going good, but there's no use now. Ok? This guy's too good to not have a key witness, there's no point. You're done."

"Captain..." Corbin quietly begged.

"And you got too many cases piling up. That's just the way it is, John. I'm sorry. Case is closed until another body shows up and even then I'm giving it to the Feds. That's all."

First Rachel, now this. No, he thought, he couldn't take another loss.

"I've never been this close."

"I know. But you don't have any more witnesses. Bring 'em in if you got 'em, but both of our jobs are on the line if you keep at this. It's a dead end. The DA has been trying to get me to give it up to the Feds for months and I'm startin' to think that's a great idea."

Detective Corbin allowed his stare to linger for a moment longer before turning and leaving the room. He considered slamming the door but thought better of it, deciding to limit the tantrums to just once today.

Morton turned to Jackson, "Take the kid to child services."

Jackson looked at him in protest, simultaneously hating the idea of driving uptown while also recognizing what that will mean for the boy's future.

"Just do it."

A moment later Captain Morton was left alone in his office. He looked through the glass and saw Jackson lean down to Kyle Sheffield. The cycle of hate and blood in this city was almost too much to handle sometimes, he thought. At least now it could be someone else's problem.

Something was wrong. The Good Samaritan found himself walking the length of MLK with the night he threatened the shopkeepers' killers racing through his mind. How did he miss it? Murderers are easy to read, they always have been. He should have known whether they needed further lessons, but he loosened his grip and an innocent man died.

Mistakes were made. I don't make mistakes, he reminded himself, never have. But something was indeed wrong. Even this night; as he wandered the streets of a neighborhood he had recently murdered an innocent woman in, this was a mistake and he knew it. But he was drawn to this place. In all his life he had never felt so exposed, so human.

Behind him he heard footsteps approaching and, without stopping, readied himself for attack. He quickly studied his surroundings: no one was ahead of him but there was an intersection thirty five feet ahead, apartments were above him with two stoops before the next block, each of the street parking spaces was occupied, one engine running, based on the sound behind him there were three men.

"Yo, boy. You got a light?"

The Good Samaritan turned to find four, not three, young men standing close enough to nearly have him half surrounded already. One of the men was barefoot, which accounted for the incorrect assessment. The first of the thugs lunged forward with a knife in his hand, The Good Samaritan pulled his own blade and sliced into his belly as he passed. All three remaining attackers learned from their friend's mistake and pushed forward in unison just as the doors swung open on the vehicle with the running engine and two more emerged.

Now five, the small army of criminals forced The Good Samaritan into the brick wall, avoiding his knife and disarming him upon impact with the hard surface. Suddenly a forearm was pushing so hard into his throat that breathing stopped. A quiet and eerily calm voice whispered into his ear.

"You know, the next time you want to slice a man up and set his mamma on fire, you should really check and see who his friends are first."

With that, The Good Samaritan felt the searing pain of a blade entering his side. The knife had gone in slowly, its wielder taking his time. These men planned to kill him slowly and were therefore patient, even with their friend bleeding out on the sidewalk. This, thought The Good Samaritan, was their second mistake.

The first had been their decision to pursue vengeance in the first place. He couldn't be sure how he found himself such an easy target, it was obviously a small community and someone must have seen him leaving the apartment that night and gotten lucky enough to spot him strolling the sidewalk. This fateful mistake masquerading as good fortune would reveal its true self over the next seventeen seconds.

If he were asked, The Good Samaritan would likely not be able to accurately recount the exact series of events as the pain radiating from his mid section was significant and blurred his awareness. Somehow he had been able to find a weakness and break free. His superior strength and instincts quickly overpowered the overly passionate young men who spent more of their energy accidentally striking each other than they did their prey. When there was just one left he looked down at his five friends who lay on the ground either dead or mortally wounded.

The boy was young, too young to really know what he was doing. He shook in fear as he slowly backed away, his pants now stained with urine. The Good Samaritan locked eyes with him and took a single step forward. In a panic, the boy sprinted away as quickly as his injured leg would carry him. The Good Samaritan stood tall until he rounded the corner at which point he allowed himself to feel the pain coming from his wound once again.

He walked to the still running vehicle his attackers had been waiting in and began the long journey to the riverside neighborhood where he could find the help he needed. The Good Samaritan managed the drive well, considering how much blood he was losing and was able to complete the drive destroying only a bare minimum of side view mirrors.

Time passed slowly as the trip seemed to take much longer than it was supposed to. The Good Samaritan had time to think, recalling the last time he had experienced this level of pain. He had already invested two years into his effort to purify the city of its evil, at which point he became obsessed with perfecting his methods. Alone in the dark recesses of his warehouse he set out to learn as much as he could about pain and the limits of the human capacity for torture. As much as he was able to, he subjected himself to various methods of incision, ripping, burning and breaking of bones.

The learning experience had been quite effective. When he healed, his next student endured a pain greater than any others and The Good Samaritan felt satisfied that the torture was significantly more efficient.

Maureen Stone had jumped out of bed when she first heard the loud knock on her door at two in the morning. Three minutes later a mass murderer was laying on her dining room table. Maureen had put on latex gloves and her eyeglasses. Antiseptic and a pile of gauze were set on the table next to needle and thread. The Good Samaritan removed his jacket and slowly lifted the white button up shirt to reveal his wound.

"Jesus," Marueen remarked as she took a closer look. "What….what happened?"

He turned to her with a look that told her she didn't want to know.

"Oh, I don't… I don't know. I mean, I'm just a nurse, I'm not a…you need a hospital."

The Good Samaritan once again shot her a silent look to remind her of what she already knew- hospitals were not an option.

"Ok, yeah yeah. Um, I mean I don't know if any organs were damaged, there's no way for me to tell for sure. All I can do is stitch you up."

She began to hyperventilate, overwhelmed from the extreme situation she suddenly found herself in. She knew she was safe from him but that didn't change the fact that the man was a killer and now whatever he had gotten involved with was her problem too. She didn't know if she could save him or if that was even the right thing to do.

The Good Samaritan reached out and held her hand, giving her a nod of confidence when she looked at him. The effort soothed her, and her breathing slowed.

After a deep sigh she said, "Ok, I'll do it. Let me clean you up first. What a mess."

Hours later The Good Samaritan awoke from a deeper sleep than he had experienced in a long time. He could barely make out any objects around him but he could tell that he was still atop Maureen Stone's dining room table. He blindly ran his fingers along the side of his abdomen until he reached the stitches, they were dry and the wound was closed but the swelling nearby was severe.

The wounded patient sat up and buttoned his shirt, as he did so Maureen stepped into the doorway and spoke cautiously, "Feeling better?"

He acknowledged her with a nod and finished buttoning his shirt before carefully tucking it in to be sure it was looking its best despite the left side being soaked with dried blood.

"Listen, I've got to go to work, so..."

Understanding, The Good Samaritan carefully stood and put on his jacket that had been slung over a dining room chair. He approached Maureen who stepped out of the way for him to exit. Pausing, he turned to her and leaned in closer than she was prepared for. His presence felt inhuman, she thought. There was something about the energy he emitted that seemed like she was looking up at some otherworldly creature that was immune to death, pain or emotion.

"Thank you," he said with a calm and sincere tone. The words of gratitude shocked her slightly. She wasn't sure what she was expecting him to say but it wasn't that. Her mind raced as he turned to leave, she had been wanting to tell him something since he knocked on her door but hadn't found the strength and it was almost too late. In a panic, she summoned the courage.

"I need you to promise me that you won't come here again."

He stopped. Without seeing his face she could sense that he was confused. He turned his head only slightly to reveal his profile.

"I'm miserable. I don't... I don't know if you even realize that, but I am." Tears formed in her eyes as she forced the words to come out. "I haven't been happy since he left. I appreciate what you did. You punished someone who needed to be punished and I appreciate...but it didn't do me any good. Not really. And having you in my house only makes it worse. I'm sorry, I just...it's not enough to stop evil men. The pain doesn't end when they die."

"I did what the police couldn't," he quietly defended himself.

"I know. I know. So that makes you better than them, but it doesn't make you some kind of a hero. Just stay away."

The Good Samaritan stood in silence for a moment. Never once did he revere himself as a hero, that was never the intention. Furthermore, he expected nothing from the people that he saved, in every way his mission was about punishing the wicked and nothing else. But her words forced him to question the good he had done.

He stepped through her front door and she quickly locked it behind him. The stolen car was still parked sloppily across the street. He would have preferred to leave it but doing so could implicate Maureen in last night's encounter.

He had a few options for locations that had been convenient in the past for disposing of or burning a car. With so much of his blood inside, it would have to be fire in order to properly purge any evidence of his involvement in what would likely be seen as a gang-related crime. He pulled out and sped down the road, questioning now more than ever what purpose he truly served in this world.

Chapter 26

The evening felt cool compared to most, certainly not cool enough to leave the windows open but just knowing that it was slightly nicer outside was helpful. John Corbin sat on his couch going through a small stack of papers, occasionally sipping a beer. Ever since the girls had come back into his life he had swapped working too late at the office for working too late at home. He had to admit that adding his children and a cold beer to the monotonous task was a considerable improvement.

Corbin briefly looked up from his work to see Jean on the other end of the couch reading a book and Bella on the carpet hunched over a stack of papers of her own, surrounded by crayons. He returned to his papers with a small smile knowing his girls were content.

The Detective had been given the red light by Morton but that couldn't stop him from pursuing hobbies at home, plus a few weeks ago he had sent a request in to the geeks in the downtown office to run their facial recognition software on The Good Samaritan. He assumed the results would be disappointing if anything came back at all but earlier that day they sent over an impressive stockpile of hits around the city.

Each camera was different, some recording at higher qualities than others, some in poor lighting conditions. Some of the recognition accuracy rated at less than 30% but still the software was impressive. Corbin had been sifting through the results and lending a human eye to remove any results that were clearly mistaken and it was incredibly satisfying to be able to, in a sense, track this man's movement throughout the city.

The results were spotty but on some days Corbin was able to track time and distance from one block to another. No matter what he always stepped into a generic black sedan and drove outside the range of the grid and never in the same direction. The information was more rewarding than he had hoped for but was still not enough to bring the case back to him.

He picked up one of the print outs featuring a close up of The Good Samaritan's face. Having seen the killer himself, he now knew that this image was the best and most accurate representation the police had. The image was grainy, having been zoomed in so far but the details were clear. At least this would be worth sharing with the FBI if they ever came to him for help.

Corbin noticed a paper hovering over his stack and looked up to see Bella offering him a look at her work with a smile. He took the paper and admired the characters; two little girls, a woman and a man in a suit with a blue tie.

"That's mommy, and me and Jean."

"Ah, I figured. And who's that good lookin' guy?" he pointed to the picture as Bella settled into his lap.

"That's you."

"Well, that's a really nice suit."

"I know, it's your favorite."

"Well, thank you, it's very nice."

These moments were happening more and more frequently. It hurt to consider the fact that he had been missing them this whole time. And for what? For something that he would never even finish. It was a spectacular waste.

Corbin's phone vibrated in his pocket, Bella fell to the couch with a giggle and he shifted his weight to retrieve it. "Hello?" he said, still smiling.

A calm voice came through the line. Someone who was skilled at delivering bad news the best way possible.

"What?" the smile on his face had vanished and a tear formed in his eye. Jean noticed the change in tone and looked up from her book. He turned to her, not knowing what to say next.

———

Nearly an hour later John Corbin found himself sitting in a chair beside Rachel's empty hospital bed. The sheets were clean and neatly tucked. The lights were low, as they always were at this time of night.

At the end of the bed sat Rachel's sister Vanessa with Jean and Bella on either side of her. The girls had their arms wrapped around their aunt, her shirt soaked with their tears. Vanessa had played her strong role at first but was soon unable to hold back her own sobs and the three of them mourned together.

John had never felt welcome in Vanessa's presence and this moment was no exception. He waited patiently, knowing that he would have the rest of his life to comfort his girls and that Vanessa would head home alone tonight.

She had been there for them when he hadn't been, and she deserved all the time she wanted.

He stood to wander the halls as his girls grieved. They say she's in a better place, he thought, that her pain has ended. He knew that was true. But this better place is somewhere far away from her girls and she must hate that she is there and they are here. This world is filled with so much hate and pain and evil but it is also filled with the ones we love. Is it better to be in a place where nothing is wrong and love is everywhere but you can't hold your children anymore?

He loved her deeply, the pain of losing her now twice was heavier than he could bear. He stayed as strong as he could for the girls on the drive home and tucked them into bed, hoping that they would sleep through the night. Jean insisted that Bella sleep in her own bed but held her little sister close as they drifted off.

Corbin slept very little, enduring frequent nightmares of The Good Samaritan's grainy image coming to life and beating him to submission. At 4am he awoke once more and determined that he was done trying to fall back asleep for the night. His bedroom door open, he could see the printed photographs that had haunted him in his dreams. Feeling the need for some closure he stood and walked to the living room.

Holding just the photographs in his hands, he slowly shuffled through them, hoping that facing his fears and acknowledging them as simple pieces of paper would prevent further nightmares. He stopped. There were at least forty five images that could be clearly identified as the killer, one had another familiar face in it.

Not believing what he was seeing, he opened his laptop and pulled up the digital copy of the photo. Corbin zoomed in on the familiar face, it was easily identifiable as Sarah Thompson. The killer was looking the other direction and did not seem to be aware of her presence as they each walked the same direction down the sidewalk about thirty feet apart.

He returned to the printed images and frantically shuffled through them. Moments later he had found two additional images on two separate dates. All three images featured her following a man who either did not know he was being watched or didn't care. She was stalking him.

John Corbin did not know what life would be like for the next few days. He had never helped to arrange a funeral or comforted two little girls during the greatest tragedy of their lives. But somehow he knew that the next day would be the last time he investigated the case of The Good Samaritan killer.

Chapter 27

It was just before dusk as the remaining sunlight streamed through the warehouse windows high above the main floor. This place, so often filled with so much pain and agony, was quite peaceful at times. The unmistakable scent of a wooden structure was enhanced on warm days as the almost living building baked in the sun. The sound proof facility was immune to the distraction of highway noise or airplanes flying overhead, instead the silence was so great that even the dust settling to the ground could be heard.

The Good Samaritan studied his home, standing before the blood stained chair that had hosted so many. Maureen's comment had shaken his faith. Warren's pitiful failure to remain without sin was a reflection of his inability to effectively teach the man. Anthony's mother, an innocent, had not deserved to die, that was emotional and rash.

He was not done with his work, he knew that. But it was clear that a lifetime of pursuing perfection had not yet been enough and there was a greater demand for improvement. He would be better. He had to be. There was no one else to do it.

At that same time, Sarah Thompson found herself questioning her own purpose in life as she looked around at the apartment and all its contents she had earned for herself. So many other products of the system were either living on the streets or were already dead. She had fought to stay above the drowning waters of her childhood and lived to see a world that wanted nothing to do with her. Her equal disdain for most of the world around her notwithstanding, she knew there was more in this life that she needed.

There was only one place to find it.

The sun had just slipped past the horizon and the asphalt was still radiating heat onto the sidewalk as she quickly made her way down her block towards the train. The warehouse was a fifteen minute ride followed by a twenty minute walk, she had made the trip dozens of times and knew the best route.

On the train, Sarah allowed herself to breathe and reflect on her continued motivations for returning to this man. She laughed lightly as she reminded herself that while her real father was a rapist it seemed that her adopted father was a murderer and boy did she have a type. She was so lost in her thoughts that she didn't notice Detective John Corbin watching her through the glass of the next train car.

He wondered why she was smiling, it seemed her emotions went back and forth quite a bit and it was often hard to get a read on her. Corbin had had a long day already and wasn't sure he was ready for how this one would end. The morning had been as hard as the night before after Jean and Bella woke. The new day brought fresh pain.

There was much to do as friends and family needed to be notified and arrangements had to be made for the service. Corbin was not required to be a part of any of it but insisted on being there as Vanessa and her parents sorted through the details. Vanessa asked if she could take the girls that night which was an incredibly fortuitous offer that Corbin gladly accepted. They would be in good hands.

The train came to a stop at the end of the line and he allowed Sarah a few seconds head start before he stepped through the sliding doors. Sarah hurried down to street level and kept a consistently fast pace as she proceeded deeper and deeper into the forgotten part of town. After fifteen minutes Corbin found himself shocked by two things; that she never looked back or even seemed to fear that she was in a dangerous part of town and that she had the stamina to move so quickly for so long. She did not strike him as an athlete and couldn't really imagine Sarah Thompson running the treadmill at the twenty four hour gym.

Street lights became less common as they sunk deeper into the warehouse district. Corbin looked around, not believing how close he had been. Sarah stepped into the gravel parking lot of a massive building that loomed nearly fifty feet in the air. She took a deep breath before pulling hard on the door to the main entrance and then closing it behind her.

Detective Corbin cautiously approached the building, removing his weapon and having it ready in his hand. The warehouse he had inspected with the help of the curious old man was just two blocks away, it was incredible how close he had come and he wondered how many other times that had happened during his investigation.

There was a vehicle parked outside, a generic black sedan. Corbin removed his phone and took a photo of the license plate and VIN number before ascending the small flight of steps that led to the front door. His hand gripped the large iron handle but he hesitated before pulling it.

Two parents in two days.

The thought crept into his mind and screamed instant regret. What if he didn't go home that night? What if they were truly orphaned? He pulled out his phone once more and sent a text to Jackson.

[Found him. 7901 91st st. Wait for confirmation.] He added the photos of the vehicle and hit 'send.'

He took a deep breath just as Sarah had done and pulled the large sliding door open which was surprisingly smooth and silent. Corbin proceeded down the long corridor, his pistol ready to fire. The place was a living nightmare, even the walls seemed to be alive. The floor was well worn but every surface was caked in dust. The rotting mattresses piled everywhere were the creepiest part, he thought, as we wondered what possible purpose they could serve.

There was shouting in the distance, he recognized the voice of Sarah Thompson. She seemed to be safe as it was her doing the shouting. Figuring that they must be on the ground floor, Corbin found a set of stairs leading to a second level, hoping to find a perspective to get a positive ID before calling in backup. They creaked slightly as he ascended but thanks to the soft surfaces of the mattresses everywhere Corbin felt sure he wasn't heard. Screams, he thought. That's why all the mattresses. The thought was disturbing.

Corbin climbed the stairs and found himself in an unused room that overlooked the main floor of the warehouse, just past the glass windows there was a catwalk made of iron. He crept out onto the metal surface and carefully hid himself in the shadows. Forty feet below him, Sarah was in tears and begging a massive man in a suit for some unknown answer. He wore a black suit and tie and sported blonde hair and piercing blue eyes.

Corbin removed his phone and sent another text message.

[Suspect confirmed. Send backup. Now.]

He rested the phone on the metal surface by his feet and held his weapon with both hands. He was never an expert marksman but had been able to make the shot at this distance more than once during training. If he were spotted he would have to put that to the test.

Suddenly a sound came from near Corbin's feet that seemed to him like a box of steel pipes dropping onto concrete. It was his phone. Jackson had responded to his text and the haptic vibrations reverberated through the iron catwalk.

[On the way. Stay safe.]

Down on the floor, The Good Samaritan immediately covered Sarah's mouth with his massive hand and turned his head so that his ear faced the direction of the catwalk. She looked at him wide eyed with confusion until he released her, grabbed a knife off the table and threw it towards the catwalk. The knife passed just inches from Corbin's face and buried itself into the wooden wall behind him.

"Get out," whispered The Good Samaritan.

"But..." Sarah protested.

"NOW!" his scream seemed to make the very building quake. She jumped back, only ever having heard his voice creep just above a whisper.

She turned and sprinted out of the room. Corbin, too, ran as fast as he could back to the unused room. Suddenly, a second knife plunged into his thigh, unable to stop his momentum he flipped over the end railing. Corbin fell onto an old piece of machinery made of aluminum which buckled on impact, his gun dropped somewhere within the recesses of the machine.

The surface was hardly a suitable safety mat but even in the moment the detective was able to be grateful it had been there as he then tumbled to the wooden floor in relative safety.

Corbin pulled the knife from his thigh as he attempted to stand. Heavy footsteps approached and he looked up to stare into the face of the monster he had been hunting for nearly three years. The Good Samaritan picked him up with incredible ease and tossed him into the center of the room just a few feet before the red chair. Corbin slowly grunted to his feet with the knife in his hand as The Good Samaritan approached.

"Is it you?" Corbin asked. He felt ashamed to be practically star struck. This man had been a concept, a fable, a myth. The experience of seeing him with his own eyes felt impossible.

"It's over, you know? They're on their way. Give up now and they'll go a little easier on you."

The Good Samaritan did not hesitate and easily avoided the knife as he struck Corbin in the ribs with his fist. Corbin surprised himself with how quickly he was able to recover and return with a swing of his own. The two men exchanged blows almost equally until Corbin's injuries exhausted him and The Good Samaritan was able to push him back followed by a powerful kick to the chest, sending the detective into the blood stained chair which toppled over on impact.

Pulling himself to his knees, Corbin noticed that the old wooden floor was shockingly smooth near the chair. The years of blood had dried into a thick layer of paint and the thought of it was possibly the most disturbing thing about the dreadful location. Corbin remembered he had come with a second weapon and pulled a small revolver from his ankle holster. He aimed and fired but was too late as The Good Samaritan was able to grab his wrist in time to redirect the shot.

The gun dropped to the floor and Corbin was again tossed across the room into the table of weapons which crashed to the floor, sending blades and other tools of torture flying all around the detective as he came to a rest on the floor.

Outside, Sarah quickly turned and entered the warehouse once more having heard the gunshot. As she closed the massive door, she noticed red and blue lights flashing in the distance.

The Good Samaritan picked up one of a dozen weapon options and placed a large, sinister looking blade against Corbin's throat. He leaned in close and whispered into the detective's ear.

"What...is...evil?"

The bizarre question confused Corbin. Suddenly, in one swift move that seemed impossibly fast, The Good Samaritan dropped the weapon, grabbed Corbin's handcuffs and chained him to a nearby pole. Corbin watched as his attacker even found the keys and tossed them out of reach.

"I heard-" Sarah stopped as she ran in and took in the situation. He was okay. "The police are coming."

The Good Samaritan looked at each of them, "Come on."

He turned and ran out of the room, Sarah followed closely behind. Around the corner, The Good Samaritan lifted a section of the floor and the two of them disappeared beneath the building. They fell into the dust of the crawl space beneath the massive warehouse. With just barely enough room to stand, she looked to him wondering what would come next. Before she could speak he grabbed her by both of her shoulders and stared into her eyes.

What she saw in his eyes was almost impossible to understand. It was sadness.

"I'm sorry," he said.

She didn't know how to respond.

"There is a white two door on the next block. Parked behind a dumpster. Keys are in the glove box. Don't follow me," he rushed in the opposite direction that he pointed her.

Inside, Corbin attempted to reach the keys when he heard the welcome sound of footsteps. A team of S.W.A.T. officers hurried in. "That way!" He directed them to The Good Samaritan's escape door.

Captain Morton approached the imprisoned detective with a small smile, happy to see his best cop alive but quietly enjoying that he had already been punished for disobeying orders.

"You okay?" he asked.

"Yeah I'm fine," Corbin winced from the pain, illustrating the half truth of his statement. "There's a car outside..."

"Yeah we got it, already got an address. The plate was a fake but the VIN was legit. We're headed over there now."

Corbin lifted his chained wrist, "Got a key?"

Morton smiled as he picked the key up off the floor and freed Corbin. His radio crackled.

"Captain, a second vehicle was spotted leaving, we lost him."

He turned to Corbin and said "Well, let's hope he's headed home then."

Twenty minutes later, Detective Corbin and Captain Morton joined a group of a dozen squad cars and S.W.A.T. outside of The Good Samaritan's home. Corbin got out and shook his head as he took in the pristine neighborhood. Killing scumbags at will seems like good money, he thought, maybe he should try it sometime.

Officers quickly exited their vehicles and hid behind them for cover with their weapons drawn, the S.W.A.T. team readied themselves to be called into action. Corbin pulled an arm sling from the med kit in the trunk and crudely applied it to his injured shoulder. He had bandaged his other wounds on the ride over, feeling confident he could have them properly dressed at a better time.

Inside the home, Lily slowly descended the stairs after seeing all the activity outside. All of the lights on the lower level were turned off and the walls flickered with red and blue flashes. She turned to see her husband at the dining room table, sitting up straight with his hands folded neatly ahead of him, his back facing the large window that opened up to the front yard.

It was quiet inside, peaceful. As Lily approached him, she could barely see his face as the flashing LEDs streaked through the glass behind him.

"What...what is this? What's going on?" she asked sheepishly.

Outside, a S.W.A.T. officer approached the captain and informed him they were ready to enter the home at any time.

"No, not yet. You don't know what this fuckin' guy's got in there. We wait. Have we confirmed that he's even inside?"

"Snipers say they have a man fitting the description through that window, sir." the officer reported.

Lily finally reached the table, standing opposite the man she loved.

"Lile, have a seat," he gestured to the chair before her.

"But what is-"

"Please. We need to talk."

She obeyed his command and sank into the wooden chair. Once again she took in the dramatic scene that had unfolded in her front yard in this peaceful neighborhood. She could see neighbors looking out their windows and stepping onto their front porch, people she would wave to every day. This can't be, she thought. What could possibly require so many of them?

"I'm scared," she said.

"I know. But you don't have to be anymore. They're here for me, I've done a lot of things that you don't know about, but that's why I'm here. You deserve to know." He spoke in a calm and patient tone.

Not sure how to respond, Lily simply waited for the next thing he planned to say.

"I'm a killer."

The words were simple. Too simple. Lily looked at him, silently begging for an explanation.

"I've killed seventy-eight people over the last thirteen years." Lily inhaled sharply as she listened. "A long time ago, a jury had freed a man that had all but been proven guilty. The evidence was all against him, his friends, even his family said he was a killer. But he knew the law and its tricks. So he got off. I found him. I took him somewhere intending to teach him a lesson. But once I started I couldn't stop, I killed him."

From behind a squad car, Morton leaned in to Corbin, "What the hell's he doing?"

Corbin was fixated on the back of The Good Samaritan's head and studied Lily's expressions as her eyes began to fill with tears.

"He's confessing," the Detective was fascinated.

At the dark wood dining table, The Good Samaritan continued. "Afterwards, my conscience got the better of me. I had made a decision that wasn't mine to make. And I wanted more. So I found another one. One just as guilty. A rapist. This time, I invited the victim to come and see for herself. She chose his fate. And that's how it has been. They all get a choice."

Lily shook her head, "It's not true. Why would you say these things, why-"

"Lily. Look outside. Do you really think that I'm lying?"

Once again she obeyed and looked beyond his shadowed face to see the force that had been summoned to her home. It had seemed incredibly excessive at first but she knew what was in the papers and on TV. He was The Good Samaritan killer.

"Why?" she asked. It was such a simple question but she knew there were no answers that would suffice. "Why do you do this?"

"It is my responsibility. To do what others are unable or unwilling to do. However, I can't say for sure why I allowed myself to first take a life. Had my father's killer been caught I'm sure I would have done things differently."

Lily's eyes widened a touch, she had heard this story before but he had only spoken of it once or twice. Her eyes begged him for an explanation.

"Yes. That was true," he offered.

She was drowning in her thoughts. He had told her about the death of his father early in their relationship and apparently the story was sincere. If he had really lost his father when he was a young man and the stories of the killer never being caught were true then how much of her life had been real? It would almost be simpler to be able to tell herself that everything was a lie instead of having to piece together this tapestry of falsehoods and authenticities.

Then something occurred to her, a thought that was possibly more terrifying than anything she had heard so far. Her mind was filled with uncertainty, as if the floor beneath her feet was disappearing while she still tried to stand on it. Thirteen years? They had been married for only ten.

"What about us?" she asked, not sure if she really wanted to know the answer. "Do you love me?"

"No."

The word hit her like a bullet. He had responded immediately without even considering the question. He allowed for another moment of silence before explaining.

"My responsibilities were attracting a lot of attention. I was careful but I had to stay off of their profile list. A married man simply doesn't fit the profile as well. I found you, I knew I could keep all of this hidden from you. Our marriage allowed me to continue my work."

Unable to hold back her sobs any longer, she began to hyperventilate and put her head on the table with her hands behind her head.

Captain Morton picked up his radio, "Ok, that's it. We're going in. Take your positions, I'll give the order." The officers readied themselves.

"It was wrong to do this to you." The Good Samaritan continued, knowing that time was running short. "That's why I'm here. You didn't deserve this, you never did. You're a good person, Lily."

She lifted her head to meet his eyes. Hearing a kind word was a welcome relief.

"So I'm giving you a choice."

He pulled Corbin's revolver from his jacket pocket and placed it on the table in front of him. Outside, the sniper announced the weapon on the radio and the tension of every officer increased immediately.

Lily couldn't stop looking at the pistol on the table. She had always hated guns and never wanted one in the house. Now she wondered what else was in her home that she didn't know about.

"You are the victim today. It's your right to decide whether I live or die." With that he picked up the pistol and held it to his head, pulling the hammer back as he did so.

The Captain stood and left the safety of his vehicle, "Whoa, whoa, whoa. Hold it! What's going on?"

Lily stared at the man who had lied to her for more than eleven years. While still hard to believe, it seemed to be true. He was a mass murderer. She had loved him truly and deeply. He had manipulated her from the first moment that he laid eyes on her. This psychopath had stolen the best years of her life and slaughtered a horrifying number of people along the way. Everything she knew was a lie.

"You should feel no guilt for my-"

"I don't want you to die."

The Good Samaritan blinked, shocked to hear her say it. He pulled the gun slightly away from his temple.

"I want you to go to jail," she lowered her voice as she stood and leaned over the table towards him, her shiny blonde curls falling down over her shoulders. "For the rest of your life. Go to jail and rot."

Unable to understand her decision, The Good Samaritan lowered the weapon to the table and gently replaced the hammer. He looked at the pistol, it felt wrong that it had not been used, then looked up to meet her tearful eyes.

On the front lawn, the Captain waited to give the order, perplexed by the turn of events. Suddenly, shouting drew his attention to the front door of the home which had opened. The Good Samaritan slowly emerged with his fingers interlaced behind his head. A small team of officers rushed to him and kicked out his knees knocking him to the ground before they tied his wrists with flex cuffs.

Lily stepped into the doorway and watched as her husband was pulled to his feet and carried away. He never looked back at her. Stepping out from behind a squad car, Detective John Corbin watched as The Good Samaritan was ushered into the S.W.A.T. vehicle and the doors were shut. He turned to Lily and studied her expression which showed sadness, anger and fear all at once.

———————

The cage was cold and large enough to fit a dozen men but it had been cleared out for the high profile suspect. Corbin dragged a chair in front of the bars and sat far enough away to be sure it was safe. The Good Samaritan sat on a bench. It bothered Corbin that he always insisted on sitting upright, as if his body was incapable of being in a relaxed state.

Corbin sunk into the chair. The day had been long. The week had been longer. The last three years had been a lifetime. It was over and the full weight of that relief suddenly washed over him. His wounds had been properly attended to, including having his shoulder popped back into place. His eye was swollen and two cuts on his face had been bandaged. The knife wound in his thigh throbbed in pain with each heartbeat but it would heal.

"So, what happened?" Corbin broke the silence. "Did I win? Or did you quit?"

The Good Samaritan stared at Corbin with his cold, blue eyes. The detective finally understood what the witnesses meant when they described those damn eyes, they were truly haunting.

"Which is it?" Corbin was not feeling patient.

"I apologize," The Good Samaritan broke his silence but Corbin was confused by the statement. "For your injuries. It was not my intention to hurt you."

Corbin found the killer's politeness offensive. "Answer the question."

They stared each other down, Corbin had thought that he would find himself respecting this man once he caught him. He had worried that it would interfere with his resolve, finally meeting the legend who had accomplished such an impossible task. But this arrogant prick was not worth his time. Not this night.

"What do you want to hear?" asked The Good Samaritan.

Corbin sighed aggressively before he stood and waved to the officer by the exterior gate. "Open up!" He stepped toward the exit.

"I've been reading transcripts of your cryptic bullshit for long enough, I won't sit here and listen to it myself," said the detective as he walked away.

The Good Samaritan took a breath before speaking. "I had no intention of ending my work."

The sudden spark of honesty forced Corbin to stop. Without facing him, he turned his head slightly to signify that he was listening.

"Had the girl not come tonight or had you not gotten involved, I would under no circumstances leave the evil of this city to benefit from the judicial system that I will soon myself benefit from."

The words were an unusual comfort to the detective.

"I would sooner die before quitting voluntarily."

Corbin allowed the final statement to soak in before he exited, leaving The Good Samaritan to sit and wait for judgment.

Chapter 28

Months later, the local news enjoyed their highest ratings in thirty years. The state prosecutor had moved quickly and ensured that a trial date was set as soon as possible. Although the accused had pleaded guilty on all counts, the attorney had insisted on bringing in as many witnesses as possible. There had been much discussion on what should be done with the few that were confirmed accessories to the murders. Most were divided on the subject as the line between victim and criminal became increasingly blurred.

Corbin ushered The Good Samaritan, in handcuffs, up the steps of the courthouse. The media crowded the team of officers that surrounded them. Beyond the media, a large crowd of people had also gathered, anxious to get a first person look at the famous "Good Samaritan Killer."

At the top of the steps, Detective Corbin and his prisoner paused and looked at each other. There was a moment of respect between them, two formidable opponents that had finally finished their war. The cameras flashed as The Good Samaritan was led through the large courthouse doors. Corbin turned to look at the crowd one last time and caught a glimpse of Sarah Thompson hidden among the many faces.

"Sarah," whispered Corbin. He had tried to find her but she had gone into hiding, abandoning her apartment and all its contents. There were no friends and no family to lean on.

The Good Samaritan heard the mention of Sarah's name and turned to see Corbin pushing his way through the crowd. Once clear of the mob, Corbin looked in every direction but Sarah was nowhere to be found. A proud smile crept onto The Good Samaritan's face as he turned and entered the courthouse.

Only thirty minutes later, The Good Samaritan had been asked to stand as his sentencing was read allowed. The judge had shown him no leniency during the trial, she was a veteran of the court and had been selected due to her reputation for harsh sentencing. The defendant had chosen to represent himself and stood alone as she spoke.

"You have pleaded guilty to one hundred and forty-three counts of kidnapping, unlawful imprisonment and inhumane treatment as well as seventy-eight counts of murder in the first degree. The counts are as follows; Alex Barns, August 2010, Ancil Deacon, September 2010, Jack Marsh, December 2010..."

The list was exhaustingly long. As the Judge continued, Corbin thought about his children who had been doing well considering the circumstances. Jean was proud to be the daughter of the man who was credited with capturing The Good Samaritan and it seemed her social status had taken a small bump. They were strong girls and would be okay, though never quite whole again without their mother. Tomorrow the trial would be over and Corbin had already planned to take some time off to focus on them and maybe even start fresh with a new church community.

"Throughout the duration of this hearing," the judge continued, "I have been witness to testimony that I shall never forget. The statements made by these witnesses and victims have condemned you far beyond what I am legally able to sentence you. Rest assured, sir, that what I decree here today will not be the end of your punishment. And so it is with no regret that I sentence you to fifty years in prison for each count in a maximum security prison, with no option for parole. May God have mercy on your soul."

She slammed her gavel with determination and stood to exit the courtroom. The media began snapping photos in a frenzy as The Good Samaritan stood to leave and begin his incarceration. He turned to survey the room and caught a glimpse of a familiar face. Lisa Harper sat near the back of the room. She smiled at him with tears in her eyes before he turned and was swallowed by the crowd of people.

———————

After leaving the courthouse, Sarah found herself in her old neighborhood. She had been avoiding it to be safe but decided enough time had passed. She assumed her apartment had been cleared out by now but wondered if she would be able to sneak in and find something they had missed so that she could have some connection to her past life. Now that she was being hunted by the police, she knew nothing would be the same.

As she passed the alley she noticed Caitlin sitting on the fire escape outside her window, her feet dangling over the edge. Sarah stopped to admire the innocent girl, feeling guilty that she had abandoned her. It was a quiet day with few cars on the street which was probably why Sarah was able to hear so clearly when Caitlin's father shouted at her through the closed window.

The window slammed open and the beast poked his head out just far enough to grab Caitlin by her shirt and drag her inside. The little girl screamed as the window shut. In a panic, Sarah ran to the fire escape and pulled down the ladder. She quickly ascended the metallic stairs and got to

Caitlin's window just in time to see her father huff his way out of Caitlin's empty bedroom.

Sarah quickly pulled her phone out of her pocket. It was a flip phone that she had picked up in case she felt the need to contact Alex Sommers, she could only hope that his legal services would still be paid for if needed. She began to dial 911 but hesitated. Aside from putting herself at risk, she asked herself if they would even show up and if they did would they even be able to get an honest cry for help from Caitlin? She would be too scared to tell them the truth.

Sarah knew she had to do something.

She lifted the window and quietly slid into the room. Another scream shot through the apartment and Sarah bolted through the door, into Caitlin's parent's room where she found the little girl pinned to the bed by her father, her clothes already torn.

"What the fuck?!" the pig jumped off the bed and lunged at the stranger in his home. Sarah quickly dodged him and used his forward motion to push his head into the wall which shattered from the impact. Caitlin's father fell to the floor in a daze. Without thinking, Sarah mounted him and beat him in the face with her right fist, harnessing more power than she realized she was capable of. After his nose had broken, she stood and looked back at Caitlin.

The innocent girl sat up, pulling her clothes together as best she could. The tears in her eyes had stopped flowing. She looked at her father in shock, then up to Sarah in amazement. Sarah didn't know what to do next but she knew what she could see in Caitlin's eyes; relief. It was the same relief she had once felt.

Caitlin's father was barely conscious as he took another look at the impossibly small person that had just assaulted him. Caitlin watched as Sarah grabbed him by the ankle and dragged his body through the door before slamming it shut. Sarah's eyes surveyed the small apartment as she realized that what she had done was only a momentary relief of Caitlin's pain. There was still just a door between the innocent girl and the beast at her feet.

Something more had to be done.

He tried to roll over and pull himself up to his knees but was knocked unconscious as Sarah swung the base of a floor lamp at his head. She pulled the extension cord from the end of the lamp and tied his wrists with a non-traditional but effective knot. There was no time to lose. She would have to move him and she worried that if the adrenaline faded she would lose her strength.

Sarah found car keys by the door and dragged the unconscious body through the doorway. Next she would have to use the freight elevator down to the garage, she thought. She hoped that she could remember which car he drove. After that, the future was a blur. Where would she take him? The warehouse was obviously not an option. The weight of her impulsive decision to suddenly emulate The Good Samaritan was beginning to weigh on her. But she had done it, so she would need to follow through. She would make him proud.

Once the pig had been dealt with, Sarah thought, she would return for Caitlin. The innocent young girl would be safe and Sarah would make sure that she did not suffer the failures of the system. Somehow, she would succeed where her hero had failed.

The Good Samaritan was led into his new home by four prison guards who knew his reputation well. They were ready for any sort of escape attempt and kept their weapons ready.

"Prisoner number twelve thirty-one being transferred," the guard announced to the gatekeeper before it buzzed and slid open.

The prisoner obeyed as he was commanded to step forward into the common area. His next stop would be to meet his new cell where he would spend the next four thousand years according to the state.

Everywhere he looked, men stood tall to assert their dominance as they glared at him. Some knew him from the news, others just saw him as fresh meat. The Good Samaritan studied them as he approached the entrance to his cell. The guard warned a few prisoners to step back as they crept closer to see their new neighbor.

The celebrity prisoner looked around at the company that surrounded him. Each of them were villains. It was a building filled with rapists, murderers and thieves.

It was a fucking buffett.

The guard reached over and unlocked The Good Samaritan's chains. A sinister grin stretched across his face.